BLOOD IN THE
BIG HATCHETS

D1811202

B ®

BERKLEY BOOKS, NEW YORK

BLOOD IN THE BIG HATCHETS

A Berkley Book / published by arrangement with
the author

PRINTING HISTORY
Berkley edition / June 1986

ISBN: 0-425-08792-1

A BERKLEY BOOK ® TM 757,375
Berkley Books are published by The Berkley Publishing Group,
200 Madison Avenue, New York, N.Y. 10016.
The name "BERKLEY" and the stylized "B" with design are trademarks
belonging to Berkley Publishing Corporation.

PRINTED IN THE UNITED STATES OF AMERICA

THERE WAS NO WARNING.

One moment the desert was empty, and the next moment a man stood from behind a small rock with a double-barrel shotgun already pressed to his shoulder. He was about twenty yards away, and Raider wasn't given the chance to make a fast draw. The man unloaded one barrel and then the second. The first blast knocked Raider back in the saddle. The second blew him clean out of the saddle onto the ground . . .

BLOOD IN THE BIG HATCHETS

CHAPTER ONE

Raider saw the smoke of the campfire a mile off. The thin wisp of white smoke rose straight up in the still desert air. He guessed that the two men were using old sun-bleached pieces of wood in their fire that would burn clean with the least amount of smoke to give them away. They would be watchful and wary. But not leery enough to eat cold food or raw meat. Or it could be a trap. They knew he would suspect an ambush if they put up a thick column of smoke. Maybe this way they thought they could trick him into riding there while they lay in wait to bushwhack him. But they were tired and hungry, and Raider knew from long experience that tired and hungry men don't trouble to lay clever traps. He was tired and hungry too. He'd be just as happy to see the last of these two hombres as they would of him.

He knew the two men were tired and hungry because they were running from him and he had been hunting them from before sunup. Now it was maybe two hours before sundown and they thought they had lost him long enough to have a bite to eat, knowing that when it came dark they no longer could chance the light of flames giving away their position. Raider didn't hang back to worry whether or not this was a trap. The two men had to quit running and stand their ground. Just as long as Raider got a crack at them, that was all he asked. To his way of thinking, one man's trap was another man's opportunity.

Spurring on his horse, he followed around in a half circle to where the plume of smoke rose in the sky. He threaded his way through whatever cover he could find in the desert, mostly rocks and thorn scrub that drew blood on his legs through his Levi's. He was a big man, standing six foot two, with broad shoulders and weathered skin. His eyes were a striking black, and he sported a big jet-black mustache. A black Stetson's brim kept the sun from his eyes. In spite of the heat, he wore a battered leather jacket. Most people would have dismissed him as a nondescript drifter, unpredictable, untrustworthy, probably dangerous. Those with sharper eyes would have spotted the fact that although his clothes looked like he had slept in them at the bottom of an arroyo—which he had—the gun on his right hip was clean, oiled, and well tended. It was a long-barrel Remington .44 revolver, with plain wood grips on the handle, far from new, but obviously a cared-for precision instrument in a dangerous trade. A Model 94 Winchester lever-action .30-30 carbine rested in his saddle scabbard.

The stalk of smoke from the desert campfire was nearer now. Men could hide themselves easily but not their horses, and he was looking among the rocks, cactuses, and thorn bushes strewed across the desert floor for the familiar shape and bulk of horseflesh. His own mount was still too far off from the campfire site to give him away by whinnying to horses that could be there. And if his own horse did neigh to another, it would warn Raider that the animal was closer to him than he expected—meaning in all likelihood a horseman was lying in wait for him.

There was no warning. One moment the desert was empty, and the next moment a man stood from behind a small rock with a double-barrel shotgun already pressed to his shoulder. He was about twenty yards away, too far for it to be likely that a quick pistol shot from the hip would hit him. Besides, Raider wasn't given the chance to make a fast draw. The man unloaded one barrel and then the second. Raider's right hand was on his pistol handle and his left arm was across his face when the first blast of shot knocked him back in the saddle. The second blast blew him clean out of the saddle onto the ground. He held on to the reins in his left hand as his rearing, bucking horse, stung by the shot, tried to escape and dragged him over the sand.

Raider hurt like hell from the shot. All over. And being dragged over the hard dry ground wasn't helping any. He held his long-barrel Remington .44 clear. Through his horse's legs he caught a momentary glance of the man stuffing cartridges into the broken-open barrels of his shotgun. Raider fired at his right boot. Missed. He got another look from under the horse's belly and fired again. This time he scored. He saw the man's right kneecap shatter. The .44 slug was a real man-stopper, almost enough to tear a dude's shin from his thigh when placed right in the hinge. Bastard might nail him yet with that shotgun, but he'd never dance on that leg again, for sure.

The busted knee brought the man down to the ground— down to Raider's level, with only the horse and maybe twenty paces over dry sand separating them. The man snapped the double barrels shut as he sank when his leg gave way. He screwed up his face from the pain he was feeling and concentrated on looking down the double barrels at the big

Pinkerton and giving him another one-two.

The hammer of the Remington .44 single-action had been thumbed back, and the heavy shooting iron was grasped effortlessly in Raider's big hand. Now was the time when a true gunfighter showed his steel. There were a thousand fast-draw artists who could hit a coin spun in the air but who would melt to wax and not hit a barn door when they themselves were under fire. Raider cussed and stirred up trouble when life went easy for him. When lead was thrown in his direction, he was often seen to smile. He took his time. He let the dude thumb back the twin hammers on the double-barrel and almost level the pipes on him before he gently squeezed his own trigger.

This bullet caught the man just below the throat. His mouth snapped shut and he looked at Raider out of his dead eyes along the barrels of the shotgun for a few seconds until his head nodded on the gun and he toppled slowly forward.

Raider stayed crouched and hung on to his wildly kicking horse, who was spooked by the sound of gunfire as well as the pain of two cartridges full of shot.

"Hush there, that was only birdshot," Raider soothed his mount. "I think the bastard must've mixed up his cartridges, so we got off light." Raider knew all about having fine shot picked out of his skin with the point of a knife. Folks thought it was funny. Everyone knew a .45 or .44 was real bad, and they felt sorry for a fella who had to have even a .25 or .22 dug out of him—but a skinful of fine shot was looked on as a joke. Raider could see the horse had no sense of humor about it either. "Whoa there. Down boy, down." He patted the flank and then the neck of the nervous horse, which was stamping his front hooves on the ground, looking wildly around with startled eyes and blowing air through widened nostrils.

Raider had no notion of the dead man's name. He

answered the descriptions, Raider decided as he looked down at him. Of course, so could a hundred other men. But this one had run from him. And when that didn't work, had tried to bushwhack him. If this wasn't the fella who had been robbing the trains, why had he run? Raider wasn't going to bend himself out of shape with such questions. He had come, this one had run, that was that. Now all he had to do was drill his partner too, bring in their corpses and the job was done.

After replacing the spent cartridges in his revolver, the Pinkerton slapped his horse on the haunch and took a running leap into the saddle. A smaller horse might have been staggered under the impact of this sudden load, but this big horse was tense, high-strung, and instead seemed to pick up a newfound confidence from the master on his back.

The second man was cooking meat over the fire. He put up his hands when he saw that the new arrival was not his buddy. He wasn't wearing a gun.

"You got food enough for two?" Raider growled at him. "Keep cooking it nice if you want to go on living."

The two men had shot a jackrabbit a couple of hours before, and their hunger had grown so strong, this man explained, they had decided to take the chance to cook it. One would be the lookout, the other cook.

Raider was fair, in that he split the roasted rabbit off the spit in half and shared it evenly, although he could have devoured the whole meal himself.

"What about Hal?" the man asked.

"He won't be needing any."

"You kill him?"

"He made a try for me," Raider said, gesturing at some of the puncture marks on his skin and leather jacket.

"Looks like he got you too. Did he get away?"

Raider took a rabbit leg out of his mouth and grinned. "I got tough skin. No, he didn't get away."

The cook didn't say too much more. He and Raider both knew he was going to be no trouble because he was afraid to die. He didn't have to ask any more questions to know that for him to fuck with Raider was for him to die.

After they had finished eating in silence and washed it down with coffee, Raider asked him, "You a local boy?"

"I been here a number of years."

"Okay, this is what I got to say to you. It's near dusk, so if you know a town near here, you'll get a chance to sleep in a bunk in its jail. If we sleep out here, I'll truss you up like a chicken and throw you in a prickly pear patch for the night. It's your choice."

"San Tomaso is maybe an hour due south of us."

Raider beamed. "You cook like shit and I hope never to drink coffee like this again, but I can't help taking a liking to you when you talk about this town. Now, if you was to disappoint me, I can always shoot you and sling you alongside your dead partner, who we'll pick up bye and bye when you show me where you've hidden your horses and your gold."

There was very little gold—no bars, just coins, along with silver coins and greenbacks.

"Fast as it came in," the man explained, "we spent it all on whiskey, gambling, and women—and we wasted the rest."

That was the kind of explanation Raider understood.

The Pinkerton had worked up a mean thirst in the desert, and he had promised his prisoner they would stop off at a saloon before he put him in the lockup. It bothered Raider none to gun down a man, but letting him die of needless thirst went against his code. It hit Raider kind of hard when he found every saloon in San Tomaso barred shut, with a big crowd outside the adobe church in the middle of one side of the plaza.

Oil lamps hung all around the one-story, flat-roofed adobe houses arranged around the usual square of this Spanish New Mexico town. On the eastern side of the square was a huge wooden cross, of pine beams, sunk in the dirt. Behind it was a square flat-roofed adobe building with no door or windows. Raider thought it was the town jail, but when he asked he was told it was the morada, which meant nothing to him.

"You have a marshal in this town?" the Pinkerton asked.

"Naw," a heavy, unshaven storekeeper told him. "Hereabouts you carry the law on your right hip. Or on the other side if it chances you're left-handed." He guffawed at his own joke. He lifted the head of the dead man slung face down across Raider's saddle, then let it fall again, and looked inquiringly up at Raider.

"I'm a Pinkerton. He was a train robber." Raider jerked his thumb at his prisoner, whose wrists were bound to his saddle horn with a length of rawhide. "This is his buddy."

The storekeeper nodded to Raider's prisoner like they were acquainted.

At this moment a crowd surged out of the church door into the plaza, which was illuminated by oil lamps. The excited people broke apart to leave a clear lane from the door. Raider heard a weird moaning hymn and the wails of flutes. Next thing a man emerged from the church door, barefoot and dressed in a torn white tunic. He was whipping his own back, first over one shoulder, then over the other, as he stumbled along and sang the eerie hymn. Others emerged after him in twos and threes, until there were close to thirty of them stumbling across the plaza, lashing themselves. The blood soaked through their thin tunics and ran down their legs and dropped to the dust at their feet. The last two men in the procession hauled a wooden cart filled with stones and hung with rattling chains. On top of the stones was placed, in a sitting position, a human skeleton holding a bow and arrow.

The storekeeper smiled at the expression on Raider's face. "These are our *penitentes*," he explained. "This is Holy Thursday. Tomorrow is Good Friday, the day on which Christ was put to death. Some of these men are the greatest sinners in these parts, and they do this as penance for their sins. Others are fulfilling promises they made if their prayers were answered."

"We got some Bible thumpers down in Arkansas," Raider said in an awed voice, "but I ain't never seen one to match these."

The storekeeper shrugged. "Save for one or two, in a week these will be back to their bad old ways."

The leader of the procession halted as he drew alongside Raider, still mounted on his horse. Those behind him crowded up, so they sometimes hit others on the head and shoulders with their whips as they flayed themselves. The leader, never pausing in lashing himself, pointed to the dead man slung over one horse. Three of the *penitentes* took the corpse off the horse, carried it to the cart at the rear of their group, and laid it on top of the stones next to the skeleton.

The leader, a gaunt man with hollow eyes and a huge hooked nose, scowled at Raider and the storekeeper. He stopped whipping himself and offered his bloody flail to the Pinkerton's prisoner. The man nodded his acceptance. Raider saw that the flail was made of braided soapweed with slivers of glass inserted along its length. The storekeeper produced a knife and cut the prisoner's bonds. The man glanced nervously at Raider, who did not respond, then dismounted and took the flail in his right hand. The leader of the *penitentes* ripped off the man's shirt and waited. Raider watched as his prisoner flicked the length of woven soapweed over his left shoulder onto his back, white as a fish's belly. The man winced and hunched his shoulders, then raised the lash for another blow. It left a long red weal on his white skin, from which blood trickled. He brought a second blow down alongside the weal left by the first and stepped into the procession of chanting, self-flagellating men. They resumed their slow course across the plaza toward the windowless building on its other side, and the sounds of the flutes wailed high in the still night air above the silent onlookers and the eerie hymn and the lashing of the flails.

Raider climbed off his horse, hitched it to a rail, and fell in behind the cart at the tail of the procession. The thirty or so *penitentes* walked around the windowless adobe building to a door hidden on its west side. Raider followed them in. Inside it was pitch black except for twelve candles. The *penitentes* prayed and beat themselves for a while. Then one candle was blown out. After more prayers, a second one was extinguished. At this rate, Raider figured he would be there at least a couple of hours if he was going to wait for all the candles to be blown out. He walked outside and around the building to the plaza again.

"Goddamn," he muttered to no one in particular. "I've had prisoners stole off me before, but not like this."

The sun was up when Raider woke next morning in the room he had found near the stables. He stretched and heard the straw crackle beneath him inside its burlap covering. He placed his feet on the earth floor and checked each boot for scorpions before he pulled them on and stood up. He hitched on his gunbelt, picked up his hat and carbine, and opened the door to the blinding spring sunshine. First thing he heard and saw was the *penitentes* singing their eerie hymn and lashing their bloody backs as they made their way across the plaza. He had no idea whether his prisoner was still among them or whether they had kept this up all night or were making a fresh start of it again today. At this moment, he didn't much care.

At an eating house, he ate fried eggs with hot green sauce

and cornbread. The chili sauce played hell with his stomach, and he quenched its fire with a quart of warm beer. There was nothing else to be had. The saloons in San Tomaso would be closed all day today.

He would have ridden out of town straightaway, except he had to account for the dead train robber's body, assuming the man he had shot the previous day was the train robber. His sidekick had called him Hal. Raider knew nothing more about him, and this was the kind of thing those gentlemen at their desks in Chicago, with their frock coats and clean fingernails, worried themselves about. It mattered nothing to those city slickers, Raider opined, that a bandit was safely under six feet of dirt. Their concern was paperwork—neatness, precision, and, above all, completeness. If Raider happened to know the middle name of the dead bandit's grandmother on his father's side, they would expect him to report it, and they, of course, would solemnly record it and place it in their files.

Raider had already decided to simplify his report by leaving out any mention of the *penitentes* and their cart, stones and skeleton. He would be corresponding for months with some desk-bound fool in Chicago in order to try to explain that. He'd say he left the body for the coyotes. Keeping it simple, he decided next to forget about the dead man's sidekick who had joined the *penitentes*. He didn't need a prisoner with his back cut to tatters, blood running down him like raindrops, singing a weird song. Besides, the train robber he was after was supposed to work alone. What he'd do was ask about town if anyone knew anything about the dead man, Hal. Probably no one would, because he was a train robber and no train ran anywhere near San Tomaso. Raider decided to wait about town to give his horse a rest, and ride out after the sun was no longer strong.

As he guessed, he found out nothing about Hal. The man

who had joined the *penitentes* was known, however, and Raider guessed he must have headed for these parts with his friend to hide out when pursued by him. Raider was told the man was still with the *penitentes*.

"Walk to the top of that hill south of the town and you'll find him," one man said.

As he climbed, Raider saw the *penitentes* on top of the hill. They had stopped whipping themselves but were still covered by blood and dust. Many of the ordinary townspeople of San Tomaso were looking on. Raider climbed some more and saw what they were all looking at. The man he had taken prisoner was nailed to a cross erected on the mountaintop. An iron stake was driven through each of his palms, and a third pierced his feet. He looked down from the cross at Raider and smiled.

Raider knew when he was beat. He headed down the hill, saddled his horse at the livery stable, and rode out into the desert in the midday sun.

CHAPTER TWO

Allan Pinkerton had founded his detective agency in 1850. He was a strict man who laid down a code of ethics for his employees and who liked to see everything done by the book. But Pinkerton was also a hardheaded Scots realist, and he knew that if he wanted the likes of Raider to work for him, he would have to ease up on his rules and regulations for certain of his operatives. He never let these men know this, of course. To them, Pinkerton was always the rigid, unbending taskmaster who demanded that procedures be followed to the letter. Yet in one way Allan Pinkerton was a proverbial Scotsman—he hated to see a penny wasted.

He was sitting behind the massive desk in his office at Pinkerton headquarters, at 191-193 Fifth Avenue in Chicago, when a Mrs. Phillips was announced.

"Did she just walk in off the street?" Pinkerton gruffly inquired in his Scottish burr.

"Yes, but she's quite elderly and seems highly respectable," his son William assured him.

"Show her in."

Mrs. Phillips was everything Pinkerton's son described her to be. She might once have been pretty, but this was now replaced by a shrewd yet kindly look and the no-nonsense manner of a woman used to having her orders obeyed.

"Let me come to the point right away, Mr. Pinkerton," she said as soon as she was seated. "My late husband had quite large landholdings among his assets. After his death a few years ago, like most widows are, I suppose, I was advised to sell off all his businesses and travel or live in Boston or Philadelphia or some such highly proper place, fitting for a woman of my station. In other words, resign myself to a life of tedium and years of boredom. So I am quite proud to say that I did not follow this advice. I have continued to conduct my late husband's enterprises, and most of them are prospering nicely under my ministrations."

"But not all of them," Allan Pinkerton brought her gently back to earth. "Which is of course what brings you to see me."

"I think my nephew may be robbing me."

"You think—"

"Exactly, Mr. Pinkerton. No more or no less. I *think* he may be cheating me. If he were in a business more easily monitored, I would flood the premises with auditors and accountants. As it is, he is on a cattle ranch in New Mexico, where I have been told that all such people as auditors are routinely shot for impertinence."

"I have heard similar tales myself, ma'am," Pinkerton agreed.

"I have fought railroad magnates who thought they could cheat me out of my stock, Mr. Pinkerton. As I mentioned before, I have other landholdings, and so I have some experience of what is involved. But two things restrain me from solving this problem. First, the inaccessibility of the ranch, which is near Hachita, in the southwestern corner of the state, just north of the Big Hatchet Mountains and the Mexican border."

Allan Pinkerton pondered over his wall map for a little time before he found the place.

She continued, "Second, I do not want my suspicions to sour my relationship with this nephew whom I have never met. I have no doubt he regards me as a money-hungry ghoul intent on tormenting him. My husband's brother died young, and he gave this boy a chance to manage the spread. Tad Phillips is his name. I have no children of my own, so this young man stands to inherit a large part of the fortune my husband left to me. So long as he has not been cheating me . . . If he has, I will fire him and cut him out of the will without a cent."

"I understand from what you say that you have no definite proof of wrongdoing on his part," Pinkerton said, "and that you feel the inconsistencies of the accounts may be part of doing business in this wild part of the country."

"That is my hope, Mr. Pinkerton."

The head of the detective agency shuffled through some papers on his desk until he found what he was looking for. "Normally I would not assign a top man to a fairly routine case such as this," he explained. "However, it so happens I have two of my best operatives in that general area, without another case near at hand. Weatherbee and Raider are their names. Fine upstanding young men. Yes, indeed. I suspect, ma'am, you are accustomed to the best. These are the best. I will confess to you that the thought of these two salaried operatives being idle is abhorrent to me."

Nobody paid much mind to the city slicker who walked in out of the afternoon sun to the cool shade of the Pioneer Saloon. Although the saloon was in the small town of Salt

Flat in West Texas, they saw all types of men pass through, and no city dude was going to draw a curious stare even if he was decked out in a fine worsted wool suit, silk vest, shirt, and necktie, with a pearl-gray derby on his head. He wasn't carrying a six-gun on his hip—and on this side of the Pecos River, that was the only thing that counted. Except that maybe he carried a derringer in one of his pockets. The leathery-faced cowhands in the Pioneer might laugh and call a derringer a woman's gun, but every man in the place had heard tell stories of sharply dressed dudes and gamblers getting the better of even the best gunslicks with those little pistols. The big six-shooter was awkward and hard to handle in comparison to those little toy guns. They couldn't hit a buffalo at twenty paces, but if the range was only a few feet over a gaming table or along a saloon bar, the miniature derringer was sure as a scorpion in the toe of a boot. Anyhow, nobody was messing with the city dude just because he wore a derby and a lemon-yellow silk vest.

Doc Weatherbee lit an Old Virginia cheroot, flicked an imaginary ash from a lapel of his worsted wool suit, and ordered a bottle of the best whiskey in the house.

"They got three kinds of whiskey in this saloon, stranger," the cowpoke next to him along the bar advised. "They got cheap, medium, and expensive. Only thing is, the barkeep draws all three kinds from the same barrel."

Doc poured the man a drink from his bottle when it arrived so he could compare the qualities. The cowhand threw it down in a single swallow and grinned. "It all tastes like coal oil to me," he averred.

After a while a young woman with straw-colored hair, blue eyes, and a determined look on her pretty face strode into the saloon. She looked uncertainly along the men standing at the bar, then smiled when her eyes rested on Doc Weatherbee. She sat herself at a table. Doc took his bottle and two glasses from the bar and joined her.

"He's not here," she said.

Doc poured her a drink. "Be patient."

She looked at him doubtfully. "Supposing he comes in, what're you going to do?"

"Talk with him, maybe."

"Persuade him to hand himself over to the marshal? I'm telling you, Doc, I saw this man with my own two eyes kill my uncle in cold blood because he refused to open the bank vault during the robbery. I saw the look on the brute's face as he pulled the trigger. It meant nothing more to him than swatting a horsefly. Now, maybe you think just because you're a Pinkerton you can walk up to him and say, 'See here, my good man, you've done wrong and now you'll have to come along with me.' Doc, this man didn't go to Harvard like you did. A Colt .45 is his lawbook, and it's got six pages in it. You told me you don't even carry a gun!"

"I rarely have the need to use one," Doc said airily. "And a gun causes an unsightly bulge in a good suit."

In spite of her concern, she had to laugh. "Women may be vain, but at least they know when to ease up. Only a man would get himself killed out of vanity."

Martha Brown had contacted the Pinkerton National Detective Agency a week before when she had accidentally seen the man who had shot her uncle in the bank robbery back in Wichita, Kansas, two years ago. She was staying with a cousin outside Salt Flat when she saw the man, whose name she learned was Goldtooth McGee. Martha's cousin pleaded with her not to get her husband involved, knowing that a professional gunhandler like Goldtooth McGee would be more than a match for him. Martha naturally agreed. The marshal of Salt Flat knew McGee, and he wasn't too interested in interfering. In his view, what McGee had done east of the Pecos didn't count for much west of the Pecos. Especially if it had happened as long ago as two years before. Hardly anyone in these parts cared to remember that far back. But Martha had loved her uncle, who had been a bank manager in Wichita, and she was determined to bring his killer to justice now that she had found him. She had some money of her own, more than enough to hire a private investigator, so she telegraphed her story to Allan Pinkerton in Chicago. She could have found herself a bounty hunter, because the bank had put out a $500 reward for the murderer, but Martha realized that this amounted to legally hiring one man to shoot another in the back. She wanted to see regular justice done, with judge and jury

"Will he know you if he comes in?" Doc Weatherbee asked.

"He might know me from seeing me here in Salt Flat," she replied, "because I come into town every day to see what he's up to. But he doesn't remember me from back in Wichita. There was quite a crowd of eyewitnesses in that bank, and they'll all step forward to identify him when he comes back in irons to face trial. McGee comes in here just about this time every day."

Doc smiled unconcernedly. "You'd make a good Pinkerton operative, Martha. You note facts, times, places. You'd be surprised how vague most people are about such things."

"I'm much more surprised at the easy way you sit back here, sipping whiskey, with no gun in your belt, expecting to apprehend a known murderer and desperado."

Doc tilted back the derby on his head and lit a fresh cheroot. He seemed so casual and sure of himself that the woman believed him when he told her not to worry because he knew what he was doing.

When Goldtooth McGee finally showed, Doc discovered that Martha Brown had not been anxious without cause. McGee was a huge, broad-shouldered rowdy with a beer belly and a full red beard. His nose was punched flat against his face, and his little pig eyes peered from his puffy face. He shoved a man aside to get to the bar and downed three glasses of rotgut faster than most men could swallow water. Then he wiped a massive paw across his big red beard and looked around him.

Martha and Doc pretended not to be looking at him. He looked at them and ran his eyes slowly over Martha's body with a drooling smile. Then he whirled on the man next to him at the bar, the one he had pushed out of his way before, whipped out his six-gun, and poked the frightened man in the gut with the barrel. The man was armed but had no chance to draw his weapon now. Doc saw him back away maybe twenty paces, against the side wall of the saloon, and hold up a silver dollar in his trembling right hand. Goldtooth McGee raised his six-shooter to eye level, snapped off a shot, and took the silver dollar out of the man's hand.

McGee ambled over to Doc with the smoking Colt .45 in his hand. "Git over there, fella, and hold up a dollar so the light makes it shine."

"I don't have a dollar to spare," Doc replied civilly.

Goldtooth grinned wide enough to display the cause of his name. "That's all right, fella. You can hold up a nickel or a dime, if you like. Course, since they're small, I might have to pare your fingernails a little while knocking the coin out of your hand."

Doc produced a nickel and held it up before McGee's face. "How about a bet of fifty dollars?"

McGee's eyes gleamed. "On what?"

"That I can knock the nickel from this lady's fingers without harming her. She can stand over there against that wall, which is a good thirty paces away, and I'll stand here. One shot and I'll do it, or the money is yours."

"Doc!" Martha gasped in shock.

Goldtooth muttered, "If this is some kind of trick . . ."

"What trick can there be?" Doc demanded. He put the nickel in Martha's fingers and raised the pale, dazed woman to her feet. "You place her against the wall yourself. To show you there's nothing in this aside from skill, I'll use your gun to do it."

Still trying to figure the angle but greedy for easy money from a city dude, the desperado reluctantly handed Doc his Colt. Doc tossed it behind the bar.

"What the hell did you do that for?" McGee bellowed and advanced on the much smaller Doc.

"To disarm you, of course," Doc answered as if he were talking to an idiot. "I would have thought that was obvious by now."

"Why?" Goldtooth roared.

"Remember a man you killed in a bank in Wichita? I'm here to arrest you for that. Weatherbee's the name. Pinkerton National Detective Agency."

"You scum! You ain't no bigger than a prairie dog! I'm going to tear you apart, limb from limb!"

He rushed at Doc, waving his huge fists in front of him and throwing wild swings into empty air. The immaculately clad Pinkerton paused to press his derby firmly down on his head, then retreated in a series of fancy steps while holding his two fists before him.

One cowhand at the bar said to the others, who had begun laughing at what they saw as Doc's cowardice, "That there's the latest scientific fisticuffs they've brought from England. I'll lay any man five dollars even money the city dude beats McGee."

Gold coins hit the bar in front of him, a dozen or more, laid by those who believed the only way to fight with knuckles was to slug it out, toe to toe.

Meanwhile Doc weaved and bobbed, backing away from

the bigger man and allowing McGee to charge and swing at will. The outlaw was having such a hell of a time roaring and cussing and making wild swings, he hardly noticed that none of his blows connected and that he was tiring fast. Doc advanced on him now, with his fists held out before him in that posture which caused much amusement along the bar. With his right fist, the Pinkerton blocked a blow to his head and shot back a straight left in reply, which caught McGee on the nose. The punch brought tears to the outlaw's eyes and temporarily blinded him, while Doc rained blows on his head and body. It was more the shock and disorientation caused by this sudden turn of events than the physical force of Weather-bee's punches which confused and unbalanced McGee. Doc caught him with a haymaker beneath the left jaw which made his knees turn to jelly. The Pinkerton danced back out of the way of a wild swing, ducked beneath a right cross, and delivered a bone-crunching uppercut directly beneath Gold-tooth's chin. A fast left caught the big outlaw in the right eye and made him stagger. Doc finished him off with a series of lefts and rights to the head. When he went, he dropped like a felled tree, bringing tables and chairs down with him onto the sawdust of the saloon floor.

For a moment, there was an awed silence. These cowhands had seen a lot of fights, but they'd never seen a heavy hitter laid low by a smaller man using the advanced fighting techniques of the boxing ring. Then they raised a whoop and a holler. Not minding that they had lost $5 on the fight—considering they had gotten value for their money—they cheered Doc and offered to send another bottle of whiskey to his table. Doc thanked them but declined. He bound McGee's wrists with a rawhide thong, then threw water in his face. After he had helped the outlaw to his feet and recovered his gun, Doc pushed him out the door ahead of him on their way to the town jail. Martha followed, with a grateful and admiring look on her face.

The marshal was willing enough to lock up Goldtooth McGee, now that the outlaw didn't have access to his six-gun. Doc telegraphed Chicago for headquarters to make arrangements for a deputy United States marshal to escort the wanted murderer back to Wichita.

He tried to persuade Martha to return with him to his hotel room, but she seemed more anxious to tell her friend the good news about McGee's capture and invited Doc along to celebrate the event.

"She lives in a ranch house just a few miles out of town," Martha said. "Ride out with me in the buckboard."

Doc agreed without too much enthusiasm.

As Martha had claimed, the place wasn't too far outside town. It was a plain-looking ranch house with an empty corral nearby and a weathered bunkhouse. Martha's friend, whose name was Susan, was a stunning brunette. Susan's husband was in Taos all week on business. The ladies made dinner and polite conversation. Doc entertained them with stories and jokes, and he listened to endless stories of the time they had been schoolgirls together back east. Susan insisted they both stay the night, since she would be alone in the ranch house with her husband away. She very respectably gave Martha and Doc separate rooms. When Doc tried to visit Martha after they had retired for the night, he found her door locked.

When he rapped gently on it, she called, "I'm sleepy."

He went back to his own room, wondering what had come over her. Was she afraid her friend would find out? It couldn't be that, since Martha had made references earlier to her physical relationship with Doc. He lay on his bed and tried to sleep. It was not long before he heard his room door open. Someone came in the room and closed the door softly again.

Doc heard the rustle of a silk nightgown drop to the floor, then felt one side of his bed sink as his visitor joined him in it.

Doc reached out and let his hand glide over a bare breast and down the sleek skin of her naked body. From her scent and touch, he knew immediately this wasn't Martha. Doc played along, pretending he believed it was her and not Susan. Perhaps this was why Martha had locked him out—she had made a gift of him to Susan! Maybe. Doc quit trying to figure it out and began to enjoy himself. He was really getting down to things when the bedroom door was opened and Martha stepped into the room with an oil lamp. Susan tried to cover her head with the bedsheet.

"My goodness, there you are," Doc said innocently. "I thought you were here in bed with me." He felt beside him beneath the covers. "Who can this be?"

Martha snapped, "Just so long as you get what you want, it doesn't make any difference to you which of us gives it to you!" She put down the oil lamp deliberately on the mantel, then stood surveying the scene, hands on hips, in her nightgown, an unfriendly look on her face.

Susan chose this moment to peer from beneath the sheet.

"Whore! Slut! Cow!" Martha screamed, and charged.

Doc rolled out of the bed to safety as he saw her come. Susan, entangled by the bedclothes, was not so fast, and Martha grabbed her by the hair and dragged her out of the bed onto the floor. Sobbing and shrieking, they tore and scratched at one another. Soon Martha's nightgown was ripped from her body, and the two naked women rolled around on the floor in combat.

Doc stepped in and managed to separate them at arm's length, while they spat and cursed at each other.

Martha yelled, "You no-good bitch! First you stole Tom Harbison from me, now you try to take Doc. I'll soon settle things with you, you Jezebel!"

"Tom Harbison never loved you!" Susan yelled back. "He admitted he always loved me!"

"Liar!" Martha screamed. She kicked Doc in the belly so that he released his hold and clawed at Susan's face.

Susan howled, lunged at Martha, and swung her halfway across the room by her hair.

Doc was plainly relieved that he had taken the kick in the belly instead of in the balls, and now he sat at the head of the bed, keeping out of their way. Besides, it was clear that they weren't fighting just over him. He had been around too long to need that kind of boost to his male pride. All the same, he wondered who the hell this Tom Harbison was. Martha had never mentioned him, and that wasn't the name of Susan's husband.

As they fought and wrestled each other on the floor, Doc noticed that Martha was sinking her teeth into Susan's ass while Susan was battering Martha's breasts. Bruised and scratched, the two women were tiring fast and resorting to name-calling once again. Doc guessed that the contact between their naked bodies was also exciting them sexually.

In a sudden burst of grappling, Susan trapped Martha between her legs in a scissor lock. She pummeled Martha with her fists, and when she saw that she had pinioned her opponent and made her almost helpless, she pulled on her tits, poked her in the cunt, and yanked on her pubic hair.

"Look at this tired cow!" Susan crowed to Doc. "She was too tired to make love with you and is such a bitch-in-the-manger, she didn't want me to! No wonder Tom Harbison threw her over for me!"

This last was too much for Martha to bear. She erupted from out of Susan's scissor lock after driving her fingers into Susan's cunt. Martha rolled on top of Susan and sat on her face. She settled herself so that Susan's head was caught between her thighs and she half smothered the other woman with her cunt. Doc could hear Susan's muffled cries and gasps as she threshed her arms and legs helplessly.

"Look who's on top now, Doc," Martha crooned. "You want me to piss on her face?"

Before Doc got a chance to reply, Susan had toppled Martha off her. Once more they tangled with each other on the floor, writhing together, their skins glistening with perspiration, arms and legs wound about each other, both sexually aroused now, aware of Doc's eyes on their struggling bodies.

Martha overcame her rival this time and ended sitting on top of her as Susan lay face down on the floor. Martha faced Susan's backside, which she began to slap as hard as she could. Meanwhile Susan sobbed and used one hand to play with herself. When Martha noticed this, she flew into a fresh rage, called her a pervert, and slapped her even harder, while Susan screamed for mercy and went right on masturbating herself.

To spite her, Martha drove her middle finger up Susan's asshole. Susan howled in pain. Martha hauled her to her feet by her hair and displayed her to Doc, finger still up her ass.

"Is this what you want?" Martha asked him. "Is this anything you would want to fuck?"

Doc wanted to be polite and say no, but his cock gave him away by standing at full attention.

"Men!" Martha shouted. "You bastards are worse than we women are!" She jerked her finger out of Susan's asshole, which made Susan howl again, and knocked her onto the bed. Then Martha lay on the bed herself and pulled Doc on top of her. He eased his member into her juicy twat. "Fuck me!" she yelled at him. "And you," she said, prodding the sobbing Susan in the side, "you can play with yourself while you watch Doc fucking me. You're not getting any, you whore!"

Martha had never responded to Doc so hotly before. Her body shuddered and spasmed beneath him as he drove his engorged member deep inside her in lustful, raunchy bursts, pausing to let her twist and buck in orgasmic ecstasy—but not too far gone not to turn, from time to time, to make sure Susan was watching her get stuffed. Martha had one last bed-shaking climax and Doc delivered his load into her in a strutting frenzy.

Doc lay back, sated, on the bed, with Martha between him and Susan. Martha caught the other woman by the hair and forced her head down between her thighs.

"You were chasing after Doc, weren't you, you slut? Well, now get down there and taste his cum if that's what you want. You can lick up all of it you can get. Do what I say, bitch!"

Doc heard the sound of Susan lapping between Martha's thighs and saw the satisfied smile on Martha's face as she said to Susan, "If only Tom Harbison could see you now!"

Doc asked, "Who's Tom Harbison?"

Martha ignored him.

As Doc watched Susan kneel between Martha's legs, he grew hard again. Martha had her eyes closed now in blissful abandon, and she didn't see him coming from behind into Susan. Doc eased his shaft into her damp, throbbing pussy and shoved it up to the hilt. As he drove into her squirming trembling hungry cunt, Martha forced her to eat pussy. All three went wild in a prolonged orgy of pleasure, the two women climaxing over and over and Doc trying to hold back his ejaculation until he thought the pressure might blow the top off his dick. He finally let go and filled Susan's quaking interior with his seed.

Doc lay back exhausted and lit an Old Virginia cheroot. The two women were playing with each other's bodies, softly and tenderly. They were laughing and whispering, and if it weren't for their scratches and bruises, it would be hard to believe they had been fighting each other only a short while ago.

Doc smiled and blew smoke at the ceiling. "Who's Tom Harbison?" he asked.

The women looked at each other and broke into laughter.

"Tom Harbison?" Martha said. "He was a real sweet guy who was with us in sixth grade when we were at school together back east."

CHAPTER THREE

Raider let his horse drink at a trailside spring and climbed out of the saddle to stretch his legs. Open rangeland stretched away behind him. To the south, foothills gradually rose into the peaks of the Big Hatchet Mountains. He knew that on the other side of the Big Hatchets the Mexican deserts stretched for hundreds of miles. Somewhere in these foothills was Hachita, an old town that had been Mexican up until the time of the Gadsden Purchase of 1853. This trail probably led to it. There wasn't much else around that the trail could lead to, and he hadn't spotted any other trails that didn't seem to be animal paths. He hadn't seen another human in a day and a half. This wasn't all bad, Raider figured, since this looked like Apache country. In places like this, a man could be best off not meeting any of his kind. He had been told that this remote area was famous for its marauding Apache bands, south-of-the-border rustlers, bandidos, and shifty-eyed drifters who had run out of other places to go. But that was how some people described every place west of the Mississippi.

After riding into the foothills, he spotted the town—a collection of adobe buildings around a dusty square. There was no hotel in the sense of that word elsewhere, only rooms with dirt floors around a courtyard in back of the Equity Bar. Raider took one of them, left his horse in the livery stable, and took a walk around. There was nothing much to see in the sun-baked afternoon. The town seemed almost empty. The interiors of the homes were dark and cool, and he felt watchful eyes on him through their open doorways. He went into the Cottonwood Inn, a place so dark it had to be lit with lamps in the afternoon. Card tables were spread about its wood floor, with more gaming tables along the walls. Some cowhands bellied up to its long bar.

"You new in town?" one man said to him as he poured a whiskey from his bottle. When Raider nodded, the man said, "My name's Phil Conners. I'm foreman out on the Lazy K ranch, out past the Double D, which is the largest spread in these parts. The Lazy K ain't no slouch though—it's getting bigger all the time."

Raider didn't identify himself as a Pinkerton. Phil Conners seemed an honest man, but even so, he might have something against the Pinkertons. Many men had had their friends killed or had them sentenced to jail terms because of the detective agency. A Pinkerton operative had to expect to be the target of those who had nothing personal against him but wanted to get back at the agency. Raider found it easier to get a job done by hiding the fact as long as possible that he was a Pinkerton. No one ever took him to be a law-enforcement man. Mostly they assumed he was a gunfighter.

"You just passing through?" Phil asked.

"I think I might rest here a little while," Raider cautiously opined.

"This ain't much of a town. Now, you take a place like Tascosa, and it's really two towns—the respectable part and hogtown. If you're in hogtown, you see a big printed sign before you go in the better part: NO SHOOTING BEYOND THIS LINE. And you better pay attention to that, because officers of the law is going to be on your ass if you try something. Trouble with Hachita is it's all one hogtown, there ain't no respectable portion."

"Don't bother me none," Raider said.

"But this town ain't all bad," Phil said, as if Raider had just said it was. "Some folks say everyone who dies in Hachita dies with his boots on and gets flung in a hole on a scrubby hillside. That ain't so. First of all, there's even been a few natural deaths here, where someone falls sick and dies without being edged over by someone else. And those who do die with their boots on, each gets interred in his own pine box in a proper graveyard, and if a preacher happens by, he even gets a real ceremony."

"That's mighty impressive," Raider replied, "and right interesting for anyone who'd come here with the idea of maybe passing on. Like you say, I may be passing through, but I ain't passing on."

They had a laugh over that and some drinks. Raider turned down a job as a cowhand at the Lazy K.

"You don't look like no rustler to me," Phil told him, "but if you ever was to start, don't come out to the Lazy K. My boys is real fast in stringing a man up."

"I'll keep that in mind. Same go for the Double D?"

Phil Conners gave him a sharp look. "Ain't none of my problem what goes on there."

Raider could see he wasn't going to learn anything about the Double D ranch and its manager, Tad Phillips, from the foreman of the Lazy K. The telegram from Chicago head-quarters assigning him to this mission had been brief and had included no details. This was fine with Raider, since he had always found that information supplied from distant sources was usually inaccurate, and anyway he preferred to find out things for himself and not have to deal with headquarters' skewed perception of things. He didn't press Phil for more information. Soon enough he'd turn up someone in town willing to badmouth Tad Phillips. This town would be no different from any other small town.

There was a stir in the saloon as a group of horsemen rode past outside. Raider saw they were cowhands, but these boys hadn't come to town to celebrate. There were maybe nine or ten of them, and they rode close together, keeping a wary eye out, their rifles resting crosswise before them on the saddle.

"You got a nice horse in the livery stable?" Phil asked. "Better go and see those boys don't take him. They look like they're going to claim they been stole from by comancheros."

"Comancheros? Indians?"

"Hell, no," Phil said. "These fellas is like you and me. They round up someone's cattle they find on the range, drive them in here, make out a fake bill of sale, then sell them bare-faced and legal as if they had reared them theirselves since they were calves. A middleman or jobber buys them at a bargain price and sells them again somewhere else, so in a few weeks the cattle change hands several times and are put out to grass again or driven north to the fattening pens. Either way their real owner never sees them again. I don't know why they're called comancheros. A Mexican word, I guess, though most of these boys is Anglos, like you and me."

Raider shrugged. "They sound like plain cattle rustlers to me."

"Naw, you don't see it at all. Rustlers drive off a couple of hundred head, sell them where they can, and head for the saloons. Comancheros is organized. They buy each other's stolen stock, move them this way and that, all the time making out bills of sale like they were regular cattle dealers. In a short time no rancher can prove anymore the cattle are his, even with his brand on their hides, because by this time probably some honest man has bought them legally, and he ain't going to hand over what is rightfully his. Best way a rancher can get his stock back is send out all his hands soon as he finds the animals gone, then these boys grab them wherever they be and bring them on home again. We got pens and corrals other end of town, and it seems these cowhands often come across their missing steers in Hachita, for some strange reason." He grinned. "What sometimes happens is the cowhands don't find nothing, so they take something themselves to pay them for their troubles, 'specially a nice horse left in the livery stable if it ain't locally owned."

"I'll wander out and take a look," Raider said. "I thank you for your advice."

"Any man generous as you with his whiskey can have as much free advice from me as he can bear."

Soon as Raider hit the plaza outside the Cottonwood Inn, the bullets began to fly. No one was shooting at him, so far as he could tell, but the bullets were zipping around like crazy, hitting off the sides of buildings and cutting through the air at different angles. The source of the firing was at the far end of the plaza, where a group of men on foot were using their rifles on the nine or ten cowhands he had seen passing earlier. Apparently these men had found the comancheros, and maybe their missing stock, too. Now they were riding hell for leather back the way they had come, with bullets whizzing around them. Some of them looked around on their horses to take parting shots at their attackers, but most simply kept their heads well down and rode like hell. None of them were hit, probably because the men on foot were shooting from the hip and not bothering to aim carefully. But they sure

as hell weren't firing harmless shots over the heads of the fleeing cowhands-these bullets were aimed low enough to hit.

After the last of the cowhands galloped away in a cloud of
dust, the shooting stopped except for two of the men, who
fired some rounds into the sky because they were feeling
good.

Phil Conners, who was now standing outside the saloon,
said to Raider, "That lot is with the Randall brothers."

"Are they comancheros?"

Phil grinned. "I wouldn't call them that to their faces."

"Well, I reckon my horse is safe enough now," Raider said
and went back inside the Cottonwood Inn.

Raider was woken in the middle of the night by much
shouting in English and Spanish. He strapped on his gun,
pulled on his boots, and came out, at more or less the same
time as everyone else in town, to see what was happening.

The marshal and two deputies were holding back the
crowd from an obese yet powerful-looking man who was
cowering against a wall in the light of half a dozen lamps.
Raider heard men say he should be hung without delay. He
had just killed his wife and had been caught while trying to
sneak out of town.

"She was a witch!" the man howled. "I had to do it! It was
the only way I could set myself free! She had me hexed!"

The ring of fat around his middle shook with fear, and he
seemed to be known to the townspeople as El Mellado, the
toothless one, which seemed to be a fairly accurate descrip-
tion except for a few green, crooked stumps on his lower jaw.

"Hang the scumbag!" one man shouted. "No real man
attacks a woman!"

"She wasn't a woman, she was a witch!" El Mellado
yelled back.

This got the crowd sufficiently interested to quiet down.

They wanted to hear more about what this supposed witch had done for him to kill her.

El Mellado was more than willing to tell them. "Other people knew about her. They saw her burn two candles placed in the form of a cross behind a door—and you all know that's always done to hex someone. Some of you here have seen her put a knife and fork in the shape of a cross on the side of a cooking pot toward which the sun sets. That's a sure sign of a witch putting a curse on someone! A short time after I married her, I saw her dig a hole in the ground and put something in it. Then she squatted over the hole, peed in it, and covered it up with dirt. When I wanted to dig it up to see what she had put there, she wouldn't let me and I let her lead me away, pretending I had lost interest. I came back in a short while later alone, just to find what she had hid there. But there was no sign any hole had been dug. Everything had disappeared. I poked with a stick, but all the ground was hard, like it hadn't been dug for years or never. But I guessed what she hid! It was her idol! An image of the devil she worshiped!"

Some men and women in the crowd were now telling their own stories about the strange behavior of Josefina, for that was the name of El Mellado's wife. It reminded Raider of what he had seen in a courtroom several times—how the anger of people toward the accused could suddenly change into sympathy for him. The townspeople were no longer threatening to lynch El Mellado. But they wanted to hear more.

"I wasn't the first she married," El Mellado told them in an awed voice. "She influenced many men to marry her, and she bewitched them all, then killed them. I came to see that I was fighting for my life against her! I'll tell you what she did to me. The day after we were wedded, she boiled a brew in a pot. I saw her put some things in it . . . yerba buena, yerba de golondrina, ocha alizama, cachara, manzanilla, and other things, some I forget, others I didn't know what they were. While this boiled, she muttered all kinds of things over it and made signs with her hands, then she let it cool until it was barely warm. She persuaded me to rub it on my private parts. As soon as I did what she asked, I felt those parts of me get very cold, and then the cold sort of spread all over my body. When she saw the look on my face, she started to laugh. I knew right then she had just done something awful to me. And ever since that day my pecker has been lying down and won't stand up no matter what."

The crowd busily discussed this among themselves, and it was generally agreed that what she had done to him was a worse crime than murder.

"What could I do?" El Mellado pleaded. Tears ran down his cheeks. "I begged her to release me from this curse she had put on me. But she would only laugh at me. Finally I could stand it no longer. I had been to healers, and they had all told me they had no power to raise this spell. I had to put an end to it. Yet I knew I could not overcome her evil force, and I realized that the only way I could break this spell was to destroy the witch who had put it on me. So I took a long knife and I stabbed her once for each of the long years I had to live under her curse." His voice rose to a hysterical shriek. "So I stabbed her nine times, and I saw her die with my own eyes. Now I am free! Free! There is nothing you can do to me! I am free!"

"No, you ain't," the marshal said in a quiet voice.

The crowd who had wanted to lynch El Mellado a short time ago now shouted at the marshal to let him go free.

"Only a judge and jury can do that," the marshal said firmly and led El Mellado away by the arm, with his two deputies watching the crowd and covering his back.

A man next to Raider said to him, "I think it's a crying

shame to put that man behind bars. What do you think, stranger?"

"It ain't a good reason for killing a woman, being a witch, they can't help all being born that way," Raider mumbled and went back to his room to get some shut-eye.

Doc Weatherbee sat calmly on the wagon, reading a newspaper, as the mule pulled it along the trail at a snail's pace. The mule picked its own course, stopping at will to drink at a stream or nibble on extra-succulent grass. If the animal delayed overlong, Doc would call "Judith" mildly, and the mule would look back at him, twitch her ears, and go back to what she had been doing, only moving forward again when she was good and ready to do so. The Studebaker wagon was in good condition and carried a large supply of medicines. The bottles rattled in their boxes at every bump in the trail. A canvas banner hung on either side of the wagon, bearing the legend: DOCTOR WEATHERBEE—HOMEOPATHIC MEDICINES—FREE CONSULTATION.

Weatherbee had bought the rig, along with Judith the mule and its stock of medicines, from a genuine physician some years before. At that time it seemed like an excellent way for him to go under cover in the field as a Pinkerton operative. There's no place on earth where a doctor is unwelcome, and even the hardest, toughest outlaws have got their aches and pains, like everyone else. No one thought to question why an itinerant physician was in any particular place—when they saw a doctor, they were too busy thinking of their own need to see one or were thanking their stars they didn't need to visit one. The disguise could not have worked better. It allowed Weatherbee to roam wherever he pleased. Yet he discovered quickly there was one drawback to this disguise—people were always asking him to cure them.

Weatherbee was a conscientious man. He did nothing by

halves. The thought of giving bad advice to sick people troubled him. So he took up the study of medicine. That was how he learned how little a physician could help a truly sick person, and also how most people's maladies were more a product of their mind than their body. All the doctor had to do was give them a few harmless pills or some tonic and tell them to take some and they would feel better. And they would! So Weatherbee got rid of all the dangerous remedies in his stock, always sent anyone really sick to a college-qualified physician, and sold everyone else brightly colored liquids and solids for their imagined ills.

This policy worked miraculous cures, particularly among women, who often claimed that Doc had only to touch them with his hand and they began to feel better. There were times when Doc's medical practice came close to interfering with his job as a Pinkerton operative. And often, after it had been revealed that he was a Pinkerton and not a medical man at all, people *still* came to him for cures.

As Judith lazed and malingered along the trail and Doc read the newspaper in the morning sunshine, occasional horsemen passed them from each direction, calling out a greeting but not stopping. Doc was pleased to see a group of cowhands on a creek at a bend in the trail. Their horses were grazing at the water's edge, and most of the men were cleaning their rifles and revolvers. Doc decided this would be a good chance of getting the lowdown about the ranches hereabouts, since his telegram from Chicago hadn't given him much to go on.

"How you boys all feeling?" he called to them in a cheery snake-oil salesman's voice. "I got stuff here to make your livers last a little longer against all that rotgut you pass through them. Cheap, too."

"We're doing all right, Doc."

"You local? This part of your spread?"

"Naw, we're just in these parts to look for lost property."

The men were grimmer than cowhands usually tend to be, and they went on very purposefully cleaning their guns. Doc wished them luck and decided to move on. A ways up the trail, he was startled when a man rode out from behind loose rocks, thinking it might be a holdup. But the man had no gun and seemed desperate for Doc's help.

"First of all, my friend," Doc started his spiel, "you should lose some weight, and I have a fine patent appetite reducer here at a reasonable price, a very reasonable price, which will help you do that. Let me see that mouth of yours. What happened to all your teeth? Never mind that. A mouthwash and breath freshener will stand you in good stead." Doc held up a bottle of greenish liquid. "I have it here on good authority that the President himself uses this—especially before conversing with ladies. Is there anything else I can help you with?"

"I need something to lift a curse off me."

"Absolutely," Doc said with confidence. "Any particular kind of curse?"

"One my wife put on me."

"They're the worst kind by far. It's going to take a strong potion to counteract that. Is this a general curse or does it affect something in particular?"

"My privates."

Doc raised his eyebrows. "Trust a woman to go for a man's most valuable part." He reached back in the wagon and produced a bottle of bright orange liquid. He wrapped the three bottles in a sheet of newspaper. "You take a sip from each of these bottles first thing every morning. Spit the green one back out, and swallow the other two. You do that and in a couple of weeks you'll be thinner, your breath will smell like a rose, and your erection will jump up so strong it will rip a hole in your pants. Three dollars, please."

The man laughed and gladly paid the money.

Doc asked him, "You know a Tad Phillips here?"

"Sure. Fine young fella manages the Double D. I hear he's got big troubles coming his way."

"Rustling?"

"Worse than that," the man said, stowing his package in a saddlebag. "But I got my own troubles to tend to. Take care, Doc."

In a few hours, toward late afternoon, Doc finally saw the town of Hachita up ahead. His information-gathering had been a bust. He liked to pride himself on often being able to uncover essential information about a case before even arriving on the scene—a feat that could infuriate some of his Pinkerton colleagues who had made less progress while on the scene. He would like to have been able to do it this time, since he was teamed up with Raider on this case, and Raider always rose to the bait and got mad as hell when Doc one-upped him. He wondered if his fellow Pinkerton had hit town yet, and if he had made any headway. An inquiry for a place to stay took him to a room behind the Equity Bar, which would turn out to be two doors from Raider's. Having left his clothes and personal items in the room, Doc set out for the livery stable with Judith and the wagon.

Judith had been in enough towns to know when chow was near, and she set out at a quick trot across the plaza. It may have been that the long journey and the heat had made her cantankerous or that she was plain hungry and in too much of a hurry to notice; in any case she refused to slow as Doc pulled back on the reins, and she cut across in front of a horse, giving the bigger animal a poke of the wagon shaft in its side and nearly unsaddling the rider.

"Damnation, you quack, what do you think you're up to?" a tall broad-shouldered man, lean and with a pockmarked face, bellowed at Doc.

Doc raised his derby and said politely, "Pardon us."

"I'll teach you to bring this filthy animal and your poison wagon into our town. I'm gonna run you right out of town to the other side, and you keep going when you get there."

He rode close to Judith and leaned down out of the saddle to grab the reins where it hung beneath her head. Judith jerked her head to the side, bared her huge yellow chisel-shaped teeth, and chomped down on the arm extended toward her. The mule's teeth clamped tight on the sleeve material of the rider's coat, missing his arm. Judith tossed her head and ripped the sleeve clean from the coat at its shoulder seams. Aware that he looked a fool minus one sleeve in an argument with a mule, and hearing the laughter of onlookers, the rider clattered angrily away on his horse. Doc had to get off the wagon to remove the cloth from Judith's mouth, which she was chewing and trying to swallow.

Raider spoke casually to Doc Weatherbee at the bar of the Cottonwood Inn, like any two strangers might exchange some words. Each knew without discussing it that they would operate independently as long as possible, approaching the case from their own personal angles—which both were proud to say were very different. After a while, when they were sure their conversation had aroused no curiosity, they began to talk in earnest.

"This is just a make-work job," Raider complained. "Nothing here to interest me. I ain't been out to the ranch yet or seen this Tad Phillips character. Reckon I'll ride out there tomorrow and ask for a job."

"I'll drive about, sell some medicine, and see what I can dig up," Doc said.

"You won't hear much. This Phillips is a clean liver. Comes into town, buys his supplies, and rides back out without playing a hand of cards, tilting a whiskey bottle, or putting a hand on one of them fine gals they have here. But I been hearing about you. That dumb mule of yours ripped off the sleeve of one of the leading citizens round these parts. That was Big Pete Caloway who nearly lost his flipper out there. He owns the Lazy K, right next to Phillips's Double D. I know his foreman, Phil Conners, and Phil says his boss is one mean son of a bitch."

Doc smiled. "When I hit town, it's nearly always you who's in the midst of some kind of fight. This time it is I who am involved in a disturbance, and I find you peaceful and friendly. That worries me, Raider. You must be getting old and mellow."

A flush of anger crossed Raider's sun-bronzed cheeks. He said nothing, knowing that if he reacted this easy, Doc would never let up on him.

Doc went on, "I saw a crazy guy out of town a ways. Know what he wanted a cure for? A curse he said his wife put on him."

Raider paid attention. "A fella with no teeth?"

"Right. You know about his wife?"

"Sure. He killed her. Marshal put him in the town jail yesterday, and this morning he had disappeared. The deputy on guard swears he didn't let him out, though I think he did—for money. The deputy claimed that in the early morning hours, when everything was dark and quiet, this figure floats in through the street door and back to El Mellado's cell. The deputy swears it was El Mellado's dead wife come back from the grave. She touched the cell door and it opened, then she led him by the hand toward the street door—he was walking on the floorboards, but she was just gliding several inches up. The deputy thought about going for his six-gun and at least plugging El Mellado, but she gave him a strange dead kind of look with her eyes, so he stayed still. I say this is bullshit and the deputy took cash to let him go. But you can't tell folks in this town something reasonable like that. They all believe in ghosts and spells and whatnot. You say he was still looking for a cure for the spell she put on him? He killed her to get rid of her and the curse. I guess he ain't cured of it if he believes she's still up and about, rescuing him and such-like."

Doc looked at Raider oddly. "You sound as if you half believe in it too."

Raider laughed. "Hell, I don't believe a word of it—not till I see something floating toward me half a foot above the ground, and then I'll run for my life!"

"I wouldn't be far behind you," Doc agreed. "But I reckon the troublemakers we're going to have to deal with will have their feet planted squarely on the ground." At the sound of many hoofbeats, Doc looked out the saloon window. "Hey, those are the cowhands I saw cleaning their guns and watering their horses at a creek on the way into town. There are twice as many of them now. I guess they were waiting for the others when I saw them. This looks like trouble to me."

Raider went to the dusty window and gazed out into the plaza. Townspeople were already moving indoors in a hurry. Raider explained to Doc about the comancheros.

Doc became alarmed. "I hope Judith will be all right at the stable."

"Don't worry. None of these guys is damn fool enough to steal that flea-bitten bag of bones."

Probably feeling safety in numbers, the twenty-five or so cowhands were riding with all the confidence of a cavalry company. They hadn't even drawn their rifles from their saddle scabbards yet, as if they expected no resistance this time because of their large force.

Raider said idly, talking to himself, "I'd knock the lead man of those jackasses out of the saddle with a single shot, and I'd bet you'd see the rest run for cover like frightened kids. There's no way that rabble is going to stick together and keep going when they come under fire. This is all a bluff."

Doc disagreed. "It looks like a pretty good bluff to me."

A handful of men came into the saloon. "Going to be a little hot down by the pens," one of them said. "Them Randalls have eight or nine hunnert head down there they brought to town in a hurry four days ago and haven't been able to sell and move 'em out yet. I reckon what was lost is just about to be found."

"Praise the Lord."

"And keep your head down, because them five Randall boys and their sidekicks ain't going to be beat out of all that stock just by someone spitting between their boots."

The men guzzled their rotgut, keeping a wary eye out the windows as they talked, not wanting to miss anything but not wanting to stop a stray bullet either by standing outside in the plaza.

Doc said to Raider, "I'm amazed you haven't managed to get mixed up in this."

"Give me time." Raider slapped the big Remington .44 on his right hip with the flat of his hand.

Doc shook his head. "The sooner we get this Tad Phillips straightened out and leave this place, the better. The trouble with a town like this is that trouble is the only entertainment anyone has."

"You think the opera might make a difference here?" Raider asked in his most serious tone.

Doc ignored him.

They heard gunfire down at one corner of the plaza, and all of a sudden the cowhands had retreated back in sight into the plaza.

The horsemen scattered as volleys of gunfire sounded behind them. They seemed unable to make up their minds whether to dismount, take cover and return the fire, or retreat and regroup for another attack. Some did one or the other, and the rest milled about firing wildly. At least one mounted cowhand hit the dust, shot in error by one of his own. Others were knocked out of the saddle by the rifle fire coming from the pens. Raider cursed and wished them all shot to pieces for their stupidity and lack of a leader. They pulled back finally, not in an organized retreat so they could counterattack, but in a full-scale rout.

The customers in the saloon whooped. "Teach those bastards to ride in and disturb us here in Hachita!"

"Kill the yella skunks!"

"Nail their balls to the walls!"

Of course none of them had said a word until they saw which way the fight was going to go.

By the time the cowhands had come opposite the Cottonwood Inn, they had lost maybe a third of their number, nine or ten men. They tried a halfhearted rally, shouting to encourage one another and firing back at the eight or nine men who had driven them into disarray. The fact that so few men had scattered them in the first place added to their shame and confusion. They threw bullets back, but they had already lost the belief that this would win their war for them, and so they had to lose. Once this attitude set in, the end came fast. The onlookers in the Cottonwood Inn were treated to the sight of a small number of experienced gunfighters beat off these angry cowpokes like flies.

Three of the cowhands bought it right outside the saloon in which the two Pinkertons stood. Doc forgot that he and Raider were supposed to hardly know each other. He nudged Raider and said, "Let's go, we've got work to do." Raider grabbed a couple of other men and heaved them out the door in front of him. Doc was already at the first man, who was lying on his back absolutely still. Doc pulled back an eyelid and gave Raider a thumbs-down. The guy Raider came to was moaning and clutching a big red patch on his right shoulder; Raider instructed the two "volunteers" to take him by the shoulders and knees back inside the saloon. Then he and Doc picked up the third man knocked off his horse as bullets whistled around them.

"Fuckers are shooting at us," Raider snarled and dropped his end of the injured man in the dust as he slapped leather. He snapped back the hammer of the .44 as its long barrel rose, squeezed his hand on the grip as he triggered off a shot. The bullet caught one of the riflemen who had been strutting in front of the others, hip-shooting with his rifle at anything that moved. The lump of flying lead smacked into his breast-bone, flattened out of shape as it splintered through bone and gristle, then turned end over end in his body cavity and ruptured his vital organs. The guy fell down and flopped in the dust.

Raider had dropped the head and shoulders of the injured man, who had only a flesh wound in the thigh. Doc helped him hop through the saloon door as Raider covered them and brazened it out against the riflemen with only a pistol. Lucky for him, only one or two of them saw what had happened, and they kept busy firing on the cowhands, reckoning they would settle this score after they had taken care of their main business. Raider followed Doc back into the bar.

"Fella with the shoulder wound's breathed his last," a wiry little man with gray mustaches and skin like leather announced.

Doc looked up from attending the other man's leg wound. "Are you sure?"

"What's a slicker like you doing questioning my judgment?" the old salt barked. "Danged if I ain't seen more men give up with their boots on than you ever cured nervous women of the vapors."

"That could be true," Doc allowed, but all the same he

came over and checked that the man was really dead.

Raider ignored them all and stood facing the door with the .44 revolver still in his right hand, hanging by his side. The shooting outside tapered off, and Raider heard one man say in a satisfied tone that the durned outsiders had lost more than half their men and this for sure would be the last the town would see of them. Then he heard another man say, in a more nervous and uncertain voice, that the Randalls were on their way toward the Cottonwood Inn. Raider cocked the hammer of his revolver, and the metallic snap caused a hush to spread around the saloon. A few drinkers on either side of him moved away, and others hurried out of his line of sight toward the door.

Five men came through the door and stood opposite Raider, with maybe eight or nine paces separating them. The barrel of Raider's revolver was still pointed to the floor, and the five men's rifles were also angled to the floor or ceiling.

"You shot one of my men," a lean, sharp-featured man with bright blue eyes said calmly. "My name's Randall, and I don't take it lightly."

Raider smiled in a friendly fashion. "Raider's the name. Pity about your man. He was shooting at me."

"Reckon he made a mistake."

"That he did," Raider said with finality.

Randall looked about him and saw the dead man on the floor, which made him smile. This changed to a scowl when he saw the leg-shot cowhand Doc had sat in a chair. As Randall's rifle barrel started to rise, Raider said in his friendliest tone, "I took the trouble to go outside and help drag that asshole in. Now, I know you ain't going to tell me my effort was wasted."

The rifle barrel dropped a few inches, and the four others glanced at the one who was doing the talking, clearly only waiting for his signal for them to start throwing lead.

Randall's blue eyes blazed for an instant, then just as suddenly turned calm and cold. "We don't have the inclination for this man-to-man standoff stuff you seem to favor, my friend. Me and my brothers are busy men—I got two of them with me here. You've made your point here today. We can respect you for that. Only from now on, don't get in our way."

CHAPTER FOUR

To someone who didn't know, these parched hills, mesas, and gullies looked as if they couldn't support more than a handful of goats. But the half-wild longhorns were hardy foragers who found thin blades of succulent grass in the shade of thorn thickets and could smell water from miles away. True, it took more than ten of these acres to support a single cow, but the landholdings of ranchers ran into many thousands of acres, and beyond that were the rangelands open to all.

Raider rode in the early morning sun, feeling the chill from the night still lingering. He was already on Double D land. To the northeast somewhere lay the Lazy K spread, less than half the size of the Double D, he had been told. To the north and west lay rangeland and wasteland. To the south and southeast, the jagged peaks and sheer rock faces of the Big Hatchet Mountains. Raider was in his element riding out on a morning like this into the solitude of the wild country.

49

He came across the Double D ranch house in a while. The ranch house itself was large, with the roof extending out into a porch on all four walls. A long low bunkhouse was situated a few hundred yards away, next to four corrals in which horses stood switching their tails at flies in the shade of a row of big cottonwoods. Two large barns stood beyond the corrals. Two ranch hands were saddling up in the open doorway of one barn, and a third was rolling a cigarette in one hand. They looked at Raider none too friendly.

He asked, "Mr. Phillips about?"

"You looking for work, fella, you see me, not Mr. Phillips." The man licked the cigarette paper and sealed it, still using only one hand in approved cowpoke style.

"I'm looking for work all right," Raider told him, "but not regular ranch work. I heard he might have some rustlers I could shoot for him."

All three of them looked Raider over carefully. None of them found anything funny in what he said. The two went back to saddling their mounts, and the third lit his cigarette before he said, "You'd better see the boss about that."

"Where is he at?"

The man blew smoke in the direction of the ranch house. "Might be a bit early for him yet. Morning's never his best time."

The two other ranch hands laughed at this. Raider thanked the man and walked his horse to the front door of the house. He tied the animal to an iron ring on a water trough and banged on the door.

"Come in, come in," a voice called wearily.

Raider went in and closed the door after him. The room was empty, yet was heavy with cigar smoke. The same voice called to him from another room, "Do you play billiards?"

Raider walked through the doorway and through the haze of smoke saw a thin unshaven man, teeth clamped on a long thin cigar, bending over the green felt of a billiard table and squinting along his cue prior to taking his shot. Holding his position, he cocked one eye at Raider and said, "You play?" When Raider shook his head, the man looked back along the cue, stabbed with the cue, and, with a pair of loud clicks, sent all three balls bouncing off the side cushions of the table. Then he stood upright and said, "Need a drink?"

"Sure."

He poured two fingers of whiskey for each of them, handed Raider his glass, and asked, "What brings you out this way?"

"Heard you had rustlers and other troubles needed taking care of."

"Rustlers and other troubles, eh? That what you heard? What kind of other troubles?"

Raider had no idea. The telegram from Chicago hadn't said what kind of troubles, and Weatherbee hadn't known either. But then, there was only one kind of trouble. "Money troubles."

The man laughed and introduced himself as Tad Phillips. "I'm always amazed how much bad news everybody in Hachita seems to know about me." He was just assuming that Raider's source was local gossip—he was obviously used to being the object of town talk and cared little about it. "Sit you down over there and refill your glass when you're ready, and I'll tell you what this money trouble is about. A month ago I was up in Deming on business. I was staying at the Phoenix Hotel, and while sitting in a chair in the lobby, I felt something behind me. I reached back and found a billfold. Inside was almost $300 in greenbacks, a bond for $100,000 payable to Nelson & Company, a letter written in unintelligible code, and business cards and other letters in the name of A. F. Able, a stockbroker on Wall Street in New York City. I checked at the desk and found that A. F. Able was a guest at the hotel and in his room at the moment, since his key was not at the desk.

"I went to his room to return the billfold. Able didn't want to let me in his room, said he didn't believe me until he checked for himself his billfold wasn't in any of his pockets. When he finally let me in, he was so grateful he tried to press $100 on me as a reward, saying this letter in the strange code was worth countless thousands to him. He sat right down there and then to work on decoding it, telling me the information had to be acted on right away.

"Next he said he had to go straightaway to the telegraph office in order to send his instructions to the New York Stock Exchange, and that since I had refused his reward he was going to invest the $100 in my name and pay me any profits from it. He wanted to know if I would still be in Deming tomorrow. I said I would. He said that was great, he would have news for me on my investment by that time. Next day he came to me and handed me $200, saying my investment had tripled in value, he had sold it and kept the $100 back. This $200 was mine—pure profit on the deal. Now, I had just sold seven hundred head of Double D cattle and put the money in the bank, so . . . Do I have to go on?"

"No," Raider said.

"I'm only the manager of this spread. Widow lady back east owns it, spends her time adding up columns of figures and mailing me long questionnaires. Hell, ranching is a way of life, not a way of getting rich quick. I try to make money fast so I can impress, and look what happens. I lose everything. From now on I stick with longhorns."

"Talking about which brings us to rustlers," Raider said nice and easy. "I'll shoot them for you, thirty dollars a head. No rustler, no bounty—all you give me is a bunk and my feed."

Tad Phillips seemed startled by this sudden hard offer. "We don't have rustler trouble here," he said uncertainly.

"That's not what I been hearing in town."

"They been doing a right share of talking about me in Hachita," Tad said, amused. "Sure, we get some head drove off now and again, but it ain't no worse on the Double D than it is on the Lazy K or most of the other spreads down here near the border. It sure ain't bad enough for me to hire a man to shoot them on a bounty arrangement—you'd make a mighty poor living on the Double D, my friend."

"If you say so, Mr. Phillips."

Unable to persuade Tad Phillips to give him a job on the ranch, Raider took his time about riding off the land. He spent the rest of the day riding the southern boundaries of the property, where its grazing ran up onto the slopes of the foothills and into the valleys at the base of the Big Hatchet Mountains. He couldn't be sure where the ranch's boundary lay, but every cow he saw bore the Double D brand, and he reasonably assumed this was all the ranch's pasturage—if these scrub-dotted, dusty hills could be called that.

Raider hadn't formed a bad impression of Phillips as a ranch manager just because he was playing billiards at seven in the morning with a cigar in his mouth and a whiskey glass at hand. Hell, people formed the wrong impression about him as a Pinkerton all the time from little things like that. Phillips was no businessman—that was plain—but then neither was Raider. But why had he lied about the rustlers? Raider had heard it said in Hachita that Phillips was in cahoots with a gang of Spanish rustlers, who sold Double D cattle to comancheros quite openly and who drove them off the ranch in broad daylight. Tad Phillips hadn't tried to explain that away to him like he had the lost money in Deming; he had just denied that the rustling was going on. A man can't explain something that ain't happening. Except Raider knew that it was, and he aimed to interfere.

He had ridden about all morning and the greater part of the afternoon before he spotted what he had been looking for— the huge plume of dust raised by a herd of driven cattle. Longhorns left to their own devices would very rarely herd close enough or move fast enough to raise a big dust cloud. These animals had been rounded up and were being driven. Of course the regular hands could be rounding up some diseased head or bringing back strays or pushing lost animals toward a waterhole—it could be any of a dozen things, and then again it could be a broad-daylight drive of stolen stock, with the rustlers grabbing all they could easily round up and putting distance between them and the ranch before darkness fell.

Raider rode fast, changing his direction every now and then so he would cut across the path of the traveling herd. He aimed to reach them before they got into the foothills, where he could easily be picked off by sniper fire. His plan was simple, and things worked just as he had planned them—he rode down at an angle toward the front of the moving herd. The steers saw him—and so did the seven men driving them. If Raider charged them now, firing shots, the four hundred or so steers would stampede to the left, away from the foothills. The two front riders on that side would have to ride for their lives to avoid being caught among the swerving, stampeding longhorns. As it was, the animals were already veering off to the left at the sight of him, but they were still moving at a fairly easy pace and thus could still be controlled by the riders on that side. The riders on the near side were waving crazily at Raider to hold back. The lead rider cantered forward to cut him off, which was exactly what Raider wanted. This way he would get to meet one of the men face to face and would be able to make up his own mind whether these were rustlers or ranch hands before he spooked the herd into a stampede.

The rider was Spanish, with long bandido mustaches. His

cross-draw gunbelt was tooled leather with silver decorations, as were his boots.

"You loco, hombre?" he shouted to Raider.

"I'm looking out for Mr. Phillips's steers, wondering why you're taking them into these hills."

"These steers don't belong to Phillips. They belong to Señor Gonzalez."

Raider looked at the herd, which was now close by. "Seems to me I see the Double D brand on their hides."

"I don't care what you see. These steers belong to Lobo Gonzalez, and where we're taking them ain't no concern of yours. You stay right still till these cows have gone by or me and my friends are going to have to do something about it."

"You and which of your friends?" Raider asked with a smile. "You better get them here fast, because I'm going to make my moves."

The rider went for his revolver, a nickel-plated Colt Peacemaker with ivory grips. Raider figured the guy had his name engraved on it in fancy script. He was fast. Allowing for the fact that a cross-draw on horseback was often quicker than a hip draw, because it was easier for a man to reach across his belly for the gun handle than it was to raise the elbow directly upward higher than it was meant to go, allowing for all this, the man was still a fast draw. Too fast for Raider to haul his long-barrel Remington .44 clear of its holster in time. So, as Raider drew, he dug his spurs into the flanks of his horse and yanked on the left rein. His horse burst forward and to the left, violently shouldering the other horse and unsaddling its rider before he could get a shot off with his Peacemaker. As he sat on his ass in the dust, Raider let him look for an instant into the barrel of the .44 before he put a contemptuous bullet into the middle of his face. The man flopped on his back, his features stove in around the bullet hole.

Raider galloped in front of the herd, emptying the remaining chambers of his six-gun and starting off the longhorns in a nervous run which took them away from the foothills and back onto the flatlands of the Double D.

The six riders made no effort to bring the herd back under control. Neither did they come after Raider or shoot at him, although he was within range of their rifles. Instead they came slowly around to pick up their downed fellow rider, catch his horse, and tie his body across the saddle.

By staying in town, Doc Weatherbee gave Judith a rest the day Raider was out on the Double D. He too had heard talk about Tad Phillips, along with gossip about nearly everyone else whose back happened to be turned. When Raider came in that evening, he and Doc had a chance to talk for a few minutes. Raider told his partner that the rustling was real and that Phillips had lied to him about it and refused to take him on as a bounty shooter.

Next morning Raider rode out in the direction of the Double D again. Weatherbee hitched Judith to the wagon and set out to sell medicines on outlying ranches among the foothills toward which the rustlers had been driving the cattle. When the word spread that Raider had killed a rustler out on the Double D, it was supposed that the dead rustler was one of Lobo Gonzalez's men. Doc was interested to hear that El Mellado was supposed to have joined the Gonzalez band of comancheros, rustlers, and bandidos that operated on both sides of the border. A visit to El Mellado would be almost like follow-up treatment for his complaint.

Doc stopped off at a few places on the way into the foothills and actually sold some medicines. On the way he learned that traders and merchants could safely journey into the foothills to deal with the Gonzalez group. Their leader, Lobo, always made it a point to pay for everything in gold and to give a safe-conduct to those who wished to trade with him. The result of this policy was that his group never lacked anything and had strong supporters among the storekeepers and tradesmen of Hachita.

Doc, who had expected to find an outlaws' hideout, was surprised to find an extensive ranch house, other smaller dwellings, outbuildings, and corrals in a cool grassy valley deep in the foothills. Women dressed in traditional Spanish style went about their chores, children played, and men rode about on horses. Doc was not surprised to hear that Lobo himself wanted to see him, because there were few settlements that did not have their medical problems.

Though *lobo* was the Spanish word for a wolf, there was nothing very fierce about the man who approached Doc and shook his hand. He was in his early thirties and was a typical southwestern gentleman in his appearance and ways. His English was good, yet had a Spanish accent, showing that it was not the language he spoke with his family and friends. The medical problem he brought to Doc's attention was tapeworms, mostly in the children. Doc had a purgative for that and sold him a whole crate of bottles, for which Lobo paid in gold.

"I was told I might see a former patient of mine out this way," Doc remarked. "Name of El Mellado."

"That man is wanted by the law, Señor Doctor. Surely you do not think I would harbor a fugitive?"

"Just in case you happen to see him," Doc said, selecting three bottles from his stock, "give him these with my compliments."

Lobo took them with a smile. "El Mellado was a friend of my father. His wife, too. Theirs is a sad story—an unhappy life together, no children. He had developed strange ideas. She was a difficult woman, and he was not much help to her while she lived. God judges such cases, not man."

Doc nodded. "It happened before I arrived in town. I met him after he broke out of jail. Or was rescued by his wife's ghost, which a lot of people seem to believe."

Lobo's laugh showed plainly that he was not one of these.

Doc chanced a question. "Man shot yesterday on the Double D one of yours?"

Gonzalez tensed. "Yes."

"I was talking to the fella last night who shot him. Raider is his name. He's been out trying to persuade Tad Phillips to pay him a bounty on every dead rustler he brings in. Phillips told him no, so I think this man Raider wanted to show he was for real. He's a big rough professional gunfighter. Have you seen him?"

Lobo shook his head. "You know this man well?"

"Well enough. And I know fifty others like him. One week they're the town marshal, the next week they've robbed the town bank and taken off. The only reason they don't do rustling or horse-thieving is that it's too much like hard work."

Gonzalez didn't smile. He was watching Doc closely. "So what has this man to say?"

"Nothing much. I imagine he's just looking for a job and he likes to work with his gun."

"Phillips said nothing to him? About us?"

Doc shook his head. "No, I understand he was out to see Phillips *before* he shot your man. The last time I saw Raider —yesterday— he said he was heading out toward the Double D again today. I would guess that he believes he's got himself a job."

"That man he killed was not rustling those steers. They were my steers, and he and the others were driving them here."

Doc shook his head firmly. "He told me he saw plain as could be the Double D brand on those steers."

Gonzalez paused a while. Then he said, "When this was

part of Mexico, my family owned part of the land that is now the Double D. Most of the rest of it was rangeland, open to all. The Lazy K was all rangeland, which was grabbed by Anglos. Our family title wasn't recognized, but folks hereabouts, both Spanish and Anglos, knew who really owned the land, and things worked themselves out all right for a while. Then the Double D was sold and the new owner didn't want to hear any of our local history. My father killed him. Next man to own the spread went broke because of the troubles. He sold it to someone else, then the owner sold it again within a year or so. This new owner was hard-assed about what happened on *his* land, so my father shot him, too. The ranch got sold again. My father was killed down in Mexico. I've been running things since. We still had this place but no land worth talking about—only hills and mountainsides the Anglos did not want. It was now my turn to claim our rights to put our cattle on our land. We had more troubles.

"Finally a railroad financier bought the Double D and put Tad Phillips in charge. I explained things to him. He didn't want trouble. We made arrangements between ourselves, and everything was peaceful. Until this loco bounty hunter comes along looking for rustlers to shoot! Those men were driving *my* cattle. Sure the steers had the Double D brand. Sometimes they have my brand. Others have other brands— I am a comanchero, and I sometimes bring cows from below the border.

"You tell this to your friend in town when you see him. You tell him also that next time we see him out this way, we shoot him. I don't want any trouble because of some stupid mistake. This time it was a mistake. Next time, we come into town after him. He is a very lucky man that I have had more than my fair share of troubles already, and I don't want more because of a stupid man like him."

"I'll tell him," Doc promised.

• • •

"He says I'm stupid?" Raider asked at the bar of the Cottonwood Inn.

"And loco," Doc confirmed.

"Who is this Gonzalez shit anyhow?"

"Not someone you want to mess with."

Raider snorted.

"The thing that interests us," Doc said, "is that it points to Phillips being honest. He wasn't afraid to admit to you he got taken by a con man in Deming. He had the good sense to make a deal with Gonzalez instead of getting in a shooting war with him and his friends, like some of the previous ranch owners have done. He's making a go of the Double D as a business, which is also more than some of the previous owners could do. He doesn't seem to have anyone gunning for him in town—no one has much good to say for him, but neither do they have anything very bad. I say we go and see him tomorrow, tell him we're Pinkertons, discuss things, and get the hell out of here to someplace more our style."

Raider shrugged. "I kinda like this place."

"You would. Are you coming out with me to see him?"

"Sure," Raider allowed.

Raider was keeping a close eye on two of Gonzalez's men who were standing at one end of the bar and looking at him from time to time. They had the look of cowhands, not gunfighters, so Raider wasn't too concerned. Still, he was careful not to turn his back on them. At the center of the bar, a noisy group gathered around the five Randall brothers, who seemed to be celebrating something and buying drinks for everyone within earshot of them. Raider had to consider he had also killed one of their men. Some others he should take care not to turn his back on . . . He was pleased to see his friend Phil Conners, foreman of the Lazy K, walk in the door, but Conners was closely followed by his boss, Big Pete Caloway, and three other men. They all stayed together and ordered a bottle of whiskey down along the bar from the Randalls.

Caloway and his men set up their own little celebration and for a while ignored the larger, noisier Randall crowd. Then Big Pete happened to bump against one of the men talking with the five Randall brothers. Words were exchanged. Big Pete put down his glass on the bar and, with a single blow, decked the other man. Two of the Randalls helped their friend up from the sawdust. Caloway turned on them.

"I don't take kindly to having my cattle stolen," Big Pete growled. "You boys have forged a bill of sale once too often. I've heard about them steers you sold over in Concepción with my Lazy K brand on their hides and the bill of sale you showed supposedly signed by me."

"You got it wrong, Caloway," one of the Randalls told him. "Them steers had the Lazy K brand all right, but I bought them fair and square as six-month-old calves while you was trailing a herd for the drive north. Your men was about to shoot the calves because they were too young to make the long haul and would be an added burden on their mothers. I remember they had been offered eleven cents a pound for the calf hides and they could use their flesh as camp meat. We offered to take them off their hands, fifty-five animals, at a dollar a head—and they would have no work to do shooting and skinning them. Your men shook hands on the deal and we separated the calves out of the herd and drove them to grasslands over by Thunder Butte. They've been there a year now, and we finally sold them off at Concepción to a trail drover there."

"What was my name doing on the bill of sale then?" Big Pete wanted to know.

"That wasn't your name," Randall said. "Your own trail boss signed it."

"Not to my knowledge, he didn't," Phil Conners, the foreman, put in.

"Seems strange he'd put down my name instead of his own," Caloway reflected.

"I'm not going to argue with you about a bit of paper," Randall shouted. "I've told you how I came by those cattle. Ain't that enough for you?"

"No, it ain't. I'm telling you, Randall, you and your brothers have bill-of-saled the last bunch of my cattle."

"Raider, you don't mind if I join you, do you?"

The beautiful woman smiled at him, and Raider eased along the bar to make room for her.

Doc Weatherbee raised his freshly brushed gray derby to her and said to Raider, "Don't you think we would be more comfortable at a table?"

The woman looked expectantly at him, so Raider could hardly say no. But sitting at a table, he could certainly not avoid introducing Doc to the woman.

"This here is Cynthia," he mumbled as they sat. To Raider's fury, Doc made a big show of introducing himself as a physician and insisted on ordering French champagne in an ice bucket. Raider stuck with rotgut.

"I'm amazed that someone like you, Raider, is friends with the likes of Dr. Weatherbee," Cynthia said.

Doc said with a smirk, "I've often found that gun-toting hombres have a respect for us medical men. Do you suppose it's because they foresee a possible sudden future need for one of us?"

Cynthia thought this was the funniest thing she had ever heard. Raider scowled. Weatherbee was at it again. Making him look foolish and awkward. Saying things before he had a chance to talk for himself. Putting words in his mouth. And stealing this woman from him. Raider had an uncomfortable feeling that what he had had to pay for, Doc would get for nothing.

Raider considered belting him. Weatherbee was already minus one tooth with the compliments of Raider's knuckles. It might be nice to knock another one out—right now, by sending a hammerhead blow across the table without warning into the smart-talking dandy's face. But Raider restrained himself and swallowed some rotgut. Beating upon Weatherbee would change nothing. The man was like a barbed fishhook—the more you pulled against it, the deeper its point sank in. Raider decided it would just give Weatherbee more ammunition to use against him if he showed he cared enough what he did with Cynthia to hit him for it. The two of them were talking together now like old friends, making him feel like he was an outsider and newcomer to the table.

Why the hell did Allan Pinkerton team him up with this womanizing no-good slick shyster? The man didn't carry a gun most of the time, which had near enough got one or both of them killed several times. Raider couldn't stand his proper ways concerning reports and legal things that had to be filed and the right and wrong ways to do things. In Raider's view, out here you did what had to be done the best way you could. What you did not do was bring along a whole way of doing things like in, say, Boston and try to impose them on folks in Amarillo. Weatherbee was all rules and regulations, spending his damn time brushing dust off himself and putting creases in his clothes instead of getting down and dirty out there with the real men. And the women loved him for it! That was the final blow Raider found hard to take. Why? What could they see in this little jaybird? It was a mystery to Raider. He took himself back to the bar after a while and pretended not to notice when Cynthia and Doc left together.

Cynthia was not a girl to waste time. Nicely primed by the champagne and Doc's sweet talk, she loosened her long red hair before the mirror in his room and slowly eased out of her black silk dress. She had nothing on underneath, and every inch of dress pulled down revealed another inch of soft creamy skin. Doc couldn't take it any longer, and he himself helped her off with the garment. Doc paused only to neatly fold his clothes and then dived into the bed alongside her.

She was hot. Just begging for it. She wanted no preliminaries, parted her legs, and guided his rigid cock inside her. Doc drove his member deep into her innermost reaches. He allowed his wet dick to slip slowly out of her wet pussy. She thrust up with her hips to meet him and he pushed hard inside her again, which made her moan with pleasure. He kept sliding in and out slowly, listening to her moans and sobs. When she was close to climaxing, she moaned louder, and he thrust harder and deeper and faster. Then her fingernails sunk into his back and she shuddered beneath him in a consuming orgasm. Doc stopped thrusting and let her warm moist pussy contract tightly on his engorged cock.

When she was finished, she lay still, breathing deeply. He thought she might be drifting off to sleep, so he started again, moving very, very slowly in and out of her.

She sighed and whispered, "More. More. I can't get enough of it."

CHAPTER FIVE

Big Pete Caloway, his ranch foreman Phil Conners, and four Lazy K cowhands crossed over the boundary line, marked by a low ridge, onto Double D land. Two of the cowhands had seen year-old steers with the Lazy K brand mixed up with other cattle and had been unable to separate them to drive them back home.

"Now if they was mixed up with Double D cattle, I'd say they was just strays and we could sort them out in time and be in no hurry about it," Big Pete was saying as they rode. "When you tell me them other steers they was with had several different brands, none of which are local, then I begin to think that someone has stashed these cattle out here on a far-off flat to eat and rest up awhile before he drives them on again. And my bet is that fella is keeping an eye on those cows while they're here."

"You figure he might object to us reclaiming our lost property?" Phil asked.

"It's something to keep in mind," Big Pete answered, loosening his rifle in its saddle scabbard.

"We didn't see nobody when we looked the cows over," one of the cowhands said.

Caloway said, "We won't see nobody either till we start moving our cows away. Then they'll show themselves soon enough."

They rode on across the scrubby hills, following arroyos and miniature ravines and circling around dense thorn thickets until they came to flatlands which still bore a sparse covering of spring grass. Later in the season, this grass would be burned off by the sun and the flatlands would revert to almost desert conditions. Caloway guessed that the Double D herds had already been driven from here toward their summer pastures near the foothills.

"My bet is Phillips ain't even in on this," Caloway said to Phil Conners. "Fella don't know his ass from his elbow."

"I don't think Tad Phillips is stealing from the Lazy K, 'cause he's a nice young fella," Conners replied. "Ain't fair though to say he's ignorant. He has to run three times as much land as you, boss, so he's spread out pretty thin, not having a good foreman and all."

"You stick around, Conners, you'll see me running more land than Phillips."

"How can you do that, boss? There ain't no room to expand the Lazy K, unless you're thinking of leveling some of them mountain ranges."

Caloway grinned. "I don't expect to move mountains. There are easier things than them to move." He left it at that and was gratified by the look of curiosity on Conners' face.

They found the cattle scattered over one corner of the flatlands, about three hundred fifty head altogether, of which Caloway counted forty-five as his own. He and the five other men rounded up all the beasts against the high bank of an arroyo. They made movable fences by stretching their lariats from horse to horse and separated out the Lazy K steers from the others by two men riding in and using their horses to cut each one off and chase him out. Conners was charged several times by one frisky longhorn, which gave him a chance to show off his horsemanship and knowledge of cattle by moving his mount out of the way only by inches and only at the last moment. The steer never managed to even scrape the horse with the sharp upcurved tips of its long spread of horns, and finally wandered along with the others, bewildered and beaten. The cowhands whooped, for there was nothing they respected or liked to see as much as some real fancy horsemanship in handling an ornery critter. Even Caloway allowed that Phil Conners might be as good as he had ever seen.

Four other steers ran out along with the forty-five Lazy K beeves, and all forty-nine were driven back toward Caloway's land. The six horsemen kept the animals in a tight bunch but did not run them, since there was no sense in causing them hardship.

"Mebbe the cook will spot one of those four strange ones next time he wants to butcher some beef," Caloway suggested.

"He will," Conners agreed.

The steers went easy and stayed together, with two men serving as outriders and the rest following along behind, shouting at the slow and lazy beasts. In most every bunch of longhorns there will be at least one contrary critter that will keep making breaks to the right or left or that will hang back in order to run against the drovers and get left behind. Conners had already beaten the contrary one in this bunch, and these beeves walked along meek as sheep. The cowhands talked to them to calm them. These were men who had ridden herds as big as three thousand all the way up into

Kansas with only a dozen men. Most of the longhorn steers would only have been roped and handled once in their lives —that was as calves, when they had been castrated and branded—so they weren't too friendly. A really dangerous one was a cow when a man happened between her and her calf. Many a good ranch hand died that way. Other dangerous ones were the rogue steers—thóse not properly castrated, maybe with half a ball, with small new-grown balls or maybe nothing at all, but crazy, mean, sneaky—much more deadly than a heavy bull. The bull is mostly content to bellow and scrape the ground and frighten off whatever it may be that bothers him. The rogue steer will seek a man out deliberately and try to kill. The cattle they were running today were just a bunch of pets. Which was probably why they had got stolen in the first place.

They were not far from the ridge dividing the Double D from the Lazy K when four horsemen rode toward them in a hurry.

"I told you they would have someone keeping watch," Caloway said with satisfaction, "and he went and got these others. Now, you men ain't heard me make any accusations about who stole my stock. I don't have to say a word, because here you see with your own eyes the thieves ride up to try to stop me and take back what is rightfully mine."

The four riders, who they identified as one of the Randall brothers and three of their men, slowed to look the moving cattle over carefully. Then they rode on to meet the men following behind.

"You got four head of ours in there among yours," Randall called to Caloway.

Big Pete grinned. "No way I had of knowing they was yours, Randall. That ain't your brand, and this ain't your land. Why should I think them four beeves belong to you?"

" 'Cause I say so."

"Now, ain't that news," Caloway said. "And I suppose you got a bill of sale to show for them."

"That's right, I have," Randall said.

"And I bet you got one all made out for my forty-five head, too. Pity for me to take them back after you went to all that trouble."

"You saying us Randalls stole your miserable cows?"

"I could be."

Randall, small, sharp-featured, calmly looked the big rancher in the eyes. "Make up your mind, Caloway. You calling us Randalls thieves?"

"Damn right, I am," Big Pete shouted. "Only thing is I can't prove it, as you well know. But you and I both know these animals ain't strays. They was took. And you and your brothers took them."

"Only one I see taking anything belonging to anyone else is you. I just caught you taking four head of ours. Turn 'em loose."

"I ain't breaking up this bunch till I get them on my own land," Caloway told him. "If I can separate them there, I'll send them back to you."

"I'll follow you to make sure I get them back."

Caloway stopped his horse and said carefully, "If you or any man of yours sets foot on my land, I'll shoot."

Randall watched him for a moment with his expressionless blue eyes and thin face, then he pulled his horse about and rode away, followed by his three men. As they rode, they talked among themselves, then suddenly changed direction.

Phil Conners shouted, "They're riding in to scatter the cattle!"

Caloway hauled his Remington repeating rifle out of its saddle scabbard, levered a shell into the chamber, and aimed at the rider nearest the herd. The bullet tore the man out of the saddle. He was dragged along by one foot in a stirrup for some yards before his body dropped onto the dust and lay still. The three other horsemen, one of them Randall, reined in and stayed near the fallen man. They pulled out their rifles.

"Don't shoot on them unless they fire on us," Big Pete warned his five men. "Catch up with the cattle and hold them together. They've started to run."

Frightened by the gunshot and the horsemen, the cattle were raising a cloud of dust as they charged across the rough ground. But the beeves were still headed in the right direction and were staying bunched together, so all Caloway and his men needed to do was tag along until the animals tired of stampeding, which would be soon if nothing else spooked them.

Rifles at the ready, the six men passed Randall and the other two. Outgunned two to one, Randall was not about to do anything. But he was making it very plain that he was holding his ground and that the dead man on the ground before him would be avenged—or at least not forgotten.

Doc Weatherbee and Raider had waited till they got a telegram from Chicago giving them permission to tell Tad Phillips that the ranch's owner had hired them to investigate him.

Phillips seemed neither surprised nor concerned by the news. "She's just doing what her husband did before her. He was my father's brother, so I guess he gave me this job out of pity or something after my dad died. But the fact I was his nephew didn't stop him checking on me all the time. And just because he found nothing, that didn't stop him from trying harder. You'd imagine he'd hired some kind of criminal the way he snooped on me. Now she's trying to do the same. Difference is, he knew what he was doing, and she doesn't. You could explain things to him, and he knew enough about business to judge what was reasonable and what wasn't. She doesn't. I have to write her long letters of explanation. Hell, most ranchers round here can barely sign their names. Then she talks to people in what she calls 'the livestock industry' —maybe someone who owns cattle pens in Chicago and has never been on a ranch in his life. Of course, that don't mean he hasn't got a hundred opinions to tell her about ranching. The less he knows about this end of the business, the more opinions he has, naturally. And she believes everything he says, and nothing I say. She wants to see a percentage growth every year, and I write her that if we get fifteen percent more rain and thus fifteen percent more grass, we'll get fifteen percent more beef. I tell her when she uses that word *growth*, which all these stock exchange people love to use, I tell her that growth down here means just what it says—it ain't got nothing to do with percentages, it's got to do with grass."

Doc laughed and said, "Maybe you're being too hard on her. You have your point of view, and she has hers. I think, though, that what she seems to find most important might surprise you. Here, read this telegram to us from head-quarters. Wagner is our contact there." He handed a Western Union telegram to Phillips, who held the paper close to his eyes to read the clerk's neat copperplate writing.

Preliminary report received that suggest the subject's business practices are honest if sometimes irregular and even at times incompetent. Rush full report. Client stresses that honesty alone is of paramount interest, that is, personal character over business acumen. As you requested, you are hereby authorized to identify yourselves to the subject and acquaint him with the client's inquiries. Client wishes you to assist subject in all possible ways, for any length of time necessary.

                                                              Wagner

Tad Phillips slapped his thigh and roared with laughter. "That's all she wants to know—whether I'm honest! I could have told her that! She doesn't even care if I make money here, just so long as I don't steal it. And all this time I've been racking my brains to come up with ways to make more money out of the Double D. If I was ever to do anything dishonest, it would be not to cheat her—as she thinks—but to raise her income from the Double D so she would know I was doing a good job. Now I find that she doesn't even worry about that!"

"Just like a woman," Raider said morosely. "When you think you're giving them what they want, you suddenly discover that it was something completely different they wanted all the time."

But Tad was smiling. "Maybe she's not so bad after all. Well, you two go ahead and file your full report. Give the lady what she paid for. I appreciate the way you've come out here and been frank with me, when I guess you didn't have to. I never cottoned onto Raider here as a Pinkerton. I might have been more suspicious of you, Doc, but not this big lug."

Today Phillips was dressed in a dressing gown, and whiskey and cigars were much in evidence.

Doc put it delicately. "You much of a horseman?"

"Only when I have to be. Come roundup, I'm out there from dawn to dusk. We just finished the spring roundup a couple of weeks ago and drove the herd toward the foothills for their summer grazing. Ain't nothing much to do now till water grows scarce and we start clearing waterholes and making sure none of the beasts die of thirst because they're stupid. Half my work here these days is writing letters to that damn woman's accountants and bankers and agricultural experts—oh yes, she's got those, too. One of them thinks I grow corn down here—I think he's got me mixed up with one of her farms someplace. So I drink some whiskey, write a little more, smoke a cigar, practice my billiards, write some more—that's what being a rancher's like when stock exchange people own the land. But I count my blessings. While we've got all these gunmen killing people down here and those Apaches going on their raids, I don't expect to see either her or her accountants arrive in the territory. Weren't for the gunfighters and Indians, they'd be looking over my shoulder at everything I do."

"I'll mention in our report that circumstances are different down here," Doc offered.

"I'd be obliged if you did. Of course they've been told that already, but they might believe it coming from you. You fellas want to eat? My housekeeper Jacinta is a great cook. You like tortillas? She makes the best."

The food was even better than Tad Phillips claimed, and they were all slowly recovering from this heavy meal in the middle of the day when Phillips sighted Big Pete Caloway through the window. Caloway was riding directly to the ranch house. He tied his horse outside, rapped on the door, and came in. He was surprised to see Doc and Raider. Phillips didn't tell him they were Pinkertons or even hint that they were anything but casual droppers-by. Big Pete told Tad about what had happened a couple of hours before.

"You better make them boys move that stock off your land," Caloway said. "You give them an inch and they'll be behaving in a week like they own those flatlands and always did. You heard the troubles those Randalls caused out on the Baker place a couple of years ago. They say old man Baker had to pay them each a hundred dollars—five hundred in all—for them to go away after he had done the charitable thing and given them a roof over their heads and winter grazing for their stock. If I catch them coming even close to my place, I'll shoot them dead. I ain't afeared of them boys, and I showed them that today. Now, you better roust them off your land before they squat on it. I don't want them as my neighbors, and there ain't no way they can sneak onto the Lazy K without my seeing them except through that back stretch across your land."

"I'll take care of it, Pete," Tad said. "It's right neighborly of you to warn me about it."

"Since I killed one of them on your land, you was going to hear about it anyway. Best thing you could do is kill a few more of them, scare them off good."

Phillips looked at him. "Ain't you going to be a bit worried from now on when you ride into town? There's five of them Randalls, one of you."

"I'll take precautions," Caloway said and made for the door.

After he had gone Raider found out from Phillips where exactly the Randalls' stock was supposed to be. "You've heard we're supposed to help you any way we can. I'll ride out that way and maybe light a fire under them."

"I think I'm the one who decides whether you help or not," Phillips said politely, but with determination. "Thanks for your offer, Raider, I'll let you know if I need help. I'll take care of this my own way."

Raider was pissed off at his attitude, so Doc eased him out of the ranch house before he started speaking his mind to Phillips.

"Goddang bastard in a dressing gown with a cigar—that ain't no way for a cattleman to be!" Raider complained as they rode away, Doc on a spiritless animal he had hired at the stables in Hachita. "I don't like the look of them Randalls nohow, and that spineless whelp in his silk dressing gown couldn't handle one of them, let alone five. Despite what he says, I'm riding out to those flatlands to take a look. You coming?"

Doc pondered a moment, then drew out the telegram from

Chicago that he had showed to Phillips. "Mmmm . . . wording is that the client wishes us to assist the subject in all possible ways. Nothing about whether the subject wishes us to assist him or not. I think it would be reasonable for me to accompany you."

"I'm glad you were able to fit it into your rules and regulations. You carrying a gun?"

"Certainly not."

"You aiming to talk them to death?"

Weatherbee gave Raider a severe look. "There will be no call for gunplay."

The cattle were still on the flatlands when the two Pinkertons arrived. They saw that the animals carried four different brands, none of them Double D or Lazy K.

Three of the Randall brothers rode up to them, along with another man. As usual they all hung back watchfully and let one brother do the talking.

"You fellas hear about the killing in town and ride all the way out here just to take a look?" Randall asked suspiciously. He was taking care not to threaten, knowing this was not the way to go with Raider.

Doc answered him, "We were with Tad Phillips at his ranch house when he got word. Thought we might drop by friendly like to see if we could help solve this misunderstanding."

"Well, you see what you came to see. Ain't no misunderstanding."

"Not on my part, there isn't," Doc agreed.

"You two fellas have been talking all the time with the wrong people," Randall informed them. "Listen for a moment to our side of things. Our daddy lost everything in South Carolina after the war. Hell, we never did have much, I suppose, but by the time them Yankee carpetbaggers had finished with us, we had nothing. So he brought his family out to Texas and died of hard work, and our mother died too the year after of a broken heart. Us five, we stuck together. We hired out as ranch hands and gradually got into dealing cattle. Ranchers down here curse us as comancheros behind our backs, but they're all willing to buy and sell—almost all of the smaller ranchers deals with us. Big spreads like the Double D and Lazy K turn up their noses at us, and they run their own drives north or get special prices from drovers for large herds. The small rancher don't have these advantages. He depends on us. Sure, the big ranchers look down on us as dirt. We don't own no land. We move here and there, live where we can, and graze our stock on public land. What's wrong with that? Listen to them big ranchers talk, you'd think there was something illegal about it."

"You go on like this, you'll just about bring tears to my eyes," Raider told him with a grin. "I guess you just can't be the same boys I thought I saw shoot down a dozen cowhands in town a while back."

"They came after us a second time to raise trouble. We didn't shoot none of them first time. And them cows they said was theirs, we bought them fair and square, and we got no cause to give them back on their say-so."

"I hear the cavalry was all set to come down here," Doc put in, "except they had more Apache trouble and couldn't come, luckily for you."

Randall smiled smugly. "We ain't nothing on the Apaches. They're real trouble."

"I'm going to give you some real friendly advice," Raider said to him gently. "Get off Double D grass."

Randall looked down at the grass beneath his boots as though Raider had ordered him to step off a door mat. Then he looked up and said, "How long you think this grass is going to last in the sun? Another two weeks, maybe three.

Phillips has already moved all his stock to his summer grazing. There ain't a single Double D animal left on these flatlands. If we hadn't come, all this grass would have been burned up by the sun and gone to waste. Is that what you want?"

"Why didn't you ask Tad Phillips for permission to graze some stock here?" Doc asked.

Randall looked at Doc with disdain. "'Cause New Mexico ain't like places you been living. A man *takes* down here, Doc, he don't ask. Only the weak ask, and the answer to them is always no. The strong take, and once they take, most folk go along with it."

"You're full of shit," Raider announced.

The two silent Randall brothers tensed at this, but the talkative one took no offense, and they relaxed again.

"When you say 'ask Phillips for permission,' you mean we should beg grass off him that he is wasting himself. Why should we beg from a man who makes deals with other comancheros? Phillips is hand-in-glove with that no-good Lobo Gonzalez. What's Phillips doing being friends with those Spanish bandidos and having no time for us, his own kind? Eh? Does that sound right to you?"

"Maybe Phillips is afraid you'll steal his cattle if he lets you close," Raider said.

"I suppose he's been listening to that murderer Caloway from the Lazy K. When we came to these flatlands, his cattle were already here. So they got mixed in with ours. Steers don't know who they belong to, they don't know they should keep apart. So Caloway was doing the same thing as us, using up Double D unwanted grass. Then he pulls this stunt on us and kills one of our men. He ain't heard the last of that."

"That ain't any concern of mine," Raider said. "What I'd like to know is when are you moving off this grass?"

"That ain't any concern of yours either," Randall snapped back.

"We're here on a peacekeeping mission," Doc said hurriedly. "It's still not too late to avoid further trouble."

"We ain't going to be moved off this grass till we're good and ready," Randall said contemptuously. "If Phillips tries to push us, I'll kill him stone dead."

Raider smiled at him pleasantly. "You'd better make sure I ain't close to you before you try anything like that."

The cattle on the flatlands stayed nervous and bunched together after having been rounded up in an arroyo. They tossed their horns and prepared to run when they saw a group of horsemen approach them. When the men hollered and fired their shooting irons in the air, the beeves broke and ran. The three hundred or so longhorns stampeded across the flatlands, tearing through torn scrub with their tough hides. The horsemen followed after them, yelling and firing into the air, causing the frightened beasts to run ever harder in blind panic. It was getting near sundown, and once these animals got scattered on the rangelands and mountains to the north, they'd be hell to find again and even harder to round up.

Phillips rode with Lobo Gonzalez and ten of Gonzalez's men, laughing at how easy it had been to sneak up and stampede the cattle off Double D land. All the Randalls could hope to do now was to try to catch up with the animals and keep them together till they slowed as it got dark, ride herd on them all night, and drive them someplace else the next day.

But Lobo Gonzalez had some ideas about that. The Randall brothers had been making trouble for him since they had come to these parts a few years before. Gonzalez had no great love for any of these Anglos—he would be happier if there were none around—but he had learned to live with them if not trust them. The Randalls were no good. They went out of their way to do dirt to him, even when it brought them no gain to do so. Lobo could understand a man doing bad to him if this man profited by it. But the Randalls' spite for him often brought more trouble on themselves than it did on him. He would cause them more grief this time by losing these cattle for them. Phillips only wanted to drive them off his land. He, Lobo, would see that they ended in the mountain gulches or scattered in the hills and mesas. The Randalls would have to show themselves soon if they hoped to save their stock, and he and his men were ready for them when they showed.

The Randalls showed. They tried to ride between the stampeding beeves and the pursuing horsemen. Lobo's men fired on them at a gallop with rifles and carbines, and although they didn't hit them, they slowed them and made it so the Randalls didn't chance riding across in front of them to block them. The Randalls and their men, seven in all, fired back. They were riding hard too, and their bullets went high or wide. When they saw it was too dangerous for them to ride across in front of the Gonzalez men, they veered in the same direction as the cattle and tried to head them off by outrunning them. But the three hundred steers were thundering along now, newly panicked by the rifle fire.

Then a lucky shot dropped one of the Randall horses. The six other riders turned back after the horse stumbled, went down on its forelegs, and fell on its side, legs kicking. The rider jumped clear of the falling horse and ran unhurt toward the nearest of his comrades and leapt up behind him on his horse.

"Julio!" Lobo Gonzalez commanded.

The young man named Julio yanked back savagely on the reins to halt his horse, raised his rifle to his shoulder, squinted along the barrel an instant, and fired. The Randall horse with two riders was slowed behind the others because of its added burden. Julio hit the man riding behind in the center of the back with one perfectly aimed shot.

The bullet snapped Jack Randall's spine, and he was dead before his body slammed into the ground behind the cantering horse.

The Randalls forgot their cattle now and turned to face their brother's slayer. Earlier one of their men had been killed—they could live with that. This time it was one of them. That was different.

"We shouldn't have done this!" Tad Phillips shouted and spurred his horse forward so he could go to the aid of the Randalls.

Lobo urged his horse alongside and caught Tad's horse by the bridle, slowed him, and brought him round. "They ain't thinking right now. They'd kill you if they got the chance," he said to Tad. Lobo called to his men, who had begun to exchange fire with the Randalls. "Let's go. Come on. Time to ride out."

They left behind them the knot of men and horses around the fallen man. The stampeding cattle had disappeared behind the shoulder of a mountain, leaving only dust hanging in the air.

Doc Weatherbee and Cynthia had taken a walk through a stand of piñon pines to a crag, above the town of Hachita, to view the sunset. One thing led to another, and Doc ran his hands over her soft skin as she lay, comfortable and pleasuring, on the soft bed of dry pine needles beneath the trees. He pressed his manhood deep within her warm receiving body, and he enjoyed his mastery over her, bringing her to shuddering climax after climax, until he could hold back no longer and let his seed flood into her. When they became aware of the outside world around them once again, it was dark.

"What are we going to do, Doc? We can't see a thing.

How will we find our way back? There are wolves out here."

Doc laughed. "I guarantee if some timber wolves show up around here, you'll find your way back to town real quick. But I'm kidding, don't be scared. I've seen a lot of wolves and heard a lot of stories about them, but I've never met a man yet who knows firsthand of anyone bit by one unless it was in a trap."

Something flitted down at them from the branches overhead and almost brushed their faces. She screamed.

"That was only a bat," Doc said, after he recovered from being a bit startled himself. "Truth of it is, Cynthia, it's a lot safer place to be, out on this hill, than in any of those saloons in town at this hour of night."

"At least you can see what's coming at you in the saloons," Cynthia said, still fearfully clutching his arm and looking into the blackness about her as if some fanged and clawed creature were about to materialize somewhere at any second.

They made their way slowly downhill by starlight, avoiding tree trunks and bushes they could see as solid masses blocking out the stars, and crashing into smaller things. Below the pines the hillside was sparsely vegetated, and although they could find no path, they made their way easily enough, with only some sliding gravel underfoot to worry about. They could now see lighted windows in the town.

"We could take a shortcut down by the graveyard if that wouldn't upset you," Doc said.

"If nothing else has got us by then, I reckon the dead people ain't going to rise up and chase us," Cynthia told him.

Soon Doc was able to see the outlines of some of the taller grave crosses and the picket fences that surrounded many individual plots. A low dry-stone wall surrounded the cemetery, and Doc and Cynthia set out to pick their way down along the outside of this wall. As they went, a part of the cemetery downhill came into view. A miner's lamp hung on a picket fence and cast a yellow glow on the graves for maybe fifteen feet around it. Doc and Cynthia stood stock still as soon as they saw the lamp. They watched and listened. There was no living thing to be seen in the circle of light, and no sound to be heard except wolves calling and answering far up in the hills behind them.

"Let's see if we can borrow that lamp to get us into town," Doc said. When Cynthia pulled back on his arm, frightened to go forward, Doc reassured her. "We'll creep down and see what's going on before we let anyone know we're here."

Keeping as quiet as they could, they painstakingly navigated along the edge of the wall in the darkness. Cynthia didn't cry out now when thorns pricked her; she was far more alarmed by what lay inside the graveyard wall than what lay outside.

She pulled Doc to a stop and whispered in his ear, "Do they have grave robbers and body snatchers out here?"

He shook his head and whispered back, "If a man here needs a dead body, he doesn't have to rob a grave—he just goes out and shoots himself a fresh one."

They approached closer until they were directly opposite the lamp, maybe fifty yards from where they stood. So far they had seen and heard nothing. Yet the lamp couldn't have been there long, for it glowed brightly, with a freshly trimmed wick and a full fuel supply.

Doc gently pushed Cynthia away from him and climbed onto the low dry-stone wall. "Hello! Anyone there?"

Silence.

"I want to borrow your lamp to find my way into town. I'll replace it on the picket fence along with a silver dollar tomorrow morning. If you don't agree, you don't have to show yourself—just shout 'no' to me and I'll be on my way."

Silence.

"If you continue to say nothing, I'll understand that you agree and I'll take the lamp."

Doc waited. There was no sound. Nothing moved. The wolves were still howling to one another up in the hills. Lighted windows in the town were small yellow squares beneath them.

"Wait here," Doc whispered to Cynthia. "That way whoever it is will think I'm alone. If something happens, you go on very quietly or hide yourself till daylight."

Cynthia was having none of this. "I'd prefer to die with you than be left out here alive all by myself," she whispered fiercely. "Forget the lamp, Doc. We found our way this far without it, we can go the rest of the way."

Doc held a cheroot before her face. "I've no matches; I need a light."

She knew it was hopeless to argue with him. "Let me come halfway with you. I'll hide while you pick up the lamp."

Doc helped her over the wall, picked his way with her among the graves, then made her stay while he went onward toward the circle of light around the lamp.

Doc knew that what he was doing was foolhardy, that Cynthia's wish to go on without the aid of the lamp made sense, but what the hell, if he had any sense he wouldn't be a Pinkerton operative in the first place. For Doc, survival was a game that had to be played like any other. He watched for movement out of the corners of his eyes, then paused before he stepped into the light and made a target of himself. At that moment he felt a sharp blow on the top of his head. The brim of his derby was pushed down onto the bridge of his nose by the force of the blow, and as his consciousness slipped away, Doc wondered how badly his hat had been damaged.

Next thing he knew, he was wrenching up the derby from over his eyes and climbing to his knees where he had fallen.

Cynthia was screaming somewhere in the darkness. Doc was dizzy and couldn't remember where he was or what had happened. He looked at the miner's lamp hanging on the picket fence that surrounded a grave as he got unsteadily to his feet. Puzzled, he read the inscription on the monument inside the fence.

> Stay here secure,
> My sacred tomb,
> Till wife or child
> Shall ask for room.

He had never heard of the man's name on the monument. No one he knew. There was screaming somewhere. Someone, a woman, was calling his name, screaming for help. His head was spinning. His derby was crushed. Doc felt grateful toward the hat, the way it had sacrificed itself in protecting his head. No expense would be too great to have it restored, which was the least he could do for a loyal hat. Was that a woman screaming close by, or were the sounds just inside his head? He looked around in the lamplight. Next to the picket fence was another grave, this one without a picket fence, little more than three feet between the head and foot markers, made of weathered wood boards, with letters burned with a hot iron into the headboard.

> TOMMY
> Mama, Papa,
> Weep not for me,
> For I am waiting
> In Heaven for thee.

Doc saw Cynthia stagger near the edge of the ring of light, being chased around the picket fences of the tombs by a man with a long knife. The yellow lamplight flashed on the steel blade. She was screaming, and the man was shouting something at her, over and over. Doc, still dizzy and wondering where he was, made out the man's words at the same time he recognized him. It was the toothless man, the jailbreaker who had murdered his wife. El Mellado.

"Witch! Witch! Free me from your curse!" El Mellado shouted this over and over as he stalked and thrust at Cynthia with the long blade.

In an instant Doc knew who Cynthia was and that she needed his help. He rushed at El Mellado, but the graves spun around and the ground rushed up to hit him in the face. He tried to struggle to his feet again but couldn't. The moment Doc realized his body could not function, his mind grew crystal clear.

"Cynthia, curse him," he shouted. "Stand up to him. Threaten him with another curse. He'll be afraid of you."

Cynthia was used to living by her wits and her body in some of the roughest saloons in some of the worst frontier towns, and she knew a good idea when she heard one. It had been Doc's influence that had caused her to leave her derringer behind. She prided herself on standing up to any man, given an equal chance. And she knew how to act, melodrama-style.

She took two steps forward into the full yellow flare of the lamp. She held her hands like claws on either side of her face, opened her eyes very wide, and ground her bared teeth. Then she hissed in a venomous way, "Come to me, Mellado, I am your wife back from the grave."

The man stopped, and his hand holding the knife sagged at the wrist.

"I have come up out of the ground to breathe on you with my rotten breath and kiss you with my dead mouth, Mellado," Cynthia said in a croaking voice. "And I have another curse for you, Mellado, but I have to touch you to make it work."

With a hoarse cry, El Mellado dropped the knife and ran into the darkness. Cynthia and Doc heard him crashing into picket fences farther and farther away.

Cynthia turned to Doc, who was standing unsteadily on his feet once more, and cackled, "If I was a real witch, Weatherbee, believe me when I say that at this present moment I would certainly lay a curse on you."

"Sorry, Cynthia," Doc said weakly and staggered.

Cynthia immediately forgot her outrage at his recklessness, which had nearly cost her her life, and rushed to him to support him before he fell. She picked up the lamp in one hand, put her other arm around Doc, and set out for town.

"My hat," Doc murmured hazily, pointing to his battered gray derby on the ground. "I can't leave my hat. It saved my life."

Cynthia cursed him, put down the lamp, propped him up as best she could, and picked up his derby. Then she picked up the lamp and set out again.

She stopped. "What makes me mad is how he could mistake me for his wife. He must have been visiting her grave here. I knew her to see her around town. She was ugly. I don't look anything like she looked. Now I know he must be crazy."

CHAPTER SIX

Greg Peppard snored beside his wife in one of the three rooms behind his hardware store on Hachita's plaza. The last of the hell-raisers had long left the saloons and stumbled away to sleep it off, and the town lay quiet in the mountain darkness for a few hours before the freighters started to load their wagons at the first light. Peppard had been in Hachita for more than thirty years, long before the bank opened, and it was common knowledge that many old-timers still stored their cash, gold, and other valuables in Peppard's large and ancient Pennsylvania-made safe. A steady man, a non-drinker who had never played a game of chance in his life, who had never been known to cheat on his wife or ever even raise his voice in anger against her, he would no doubt have been a regular churchgoer had there been any church in Hachita besides the Spanish-language old Catholic mission, and he was trusted by many more than the bank owner, who had been in town only seventeen years.

Peppard snored. Neither he nor his wife heard the sound of the rusty hinges giving way beneath the force of two men's shoulders thrown simultaneously against the door. The four intruders followed the sound of the storekeeper's snores. His wife woke as soon as they walked in the room, but one of them had to shake him roughly by the shoulder several times before he opened his eyes.

"Light a lamp," one man ordered Mrs. Peppard.

When the light came on, the storekeeper and his wife found themselves staring at pistols and at faces half hidden behind bandannas.

"Open your safe," one of the four ordered.

"You goddamn no-account bastards don't tell me what to do," Greg Peppard growled at them.

One of the men cracked him across the side of the head with his .45. Peppard sank to his knees, clutching his head. Mrs. Peppard rushed at the man who had hit her husband and clawed him in the face with her nails, knocking down the bandanna from his face.

"Frank Randall!" she had time to gasp before he knocked her cold with a brutal punch.

They dragged Greg Peppard to his feet. "Open your safe."

"No way. You're going to kill me anyhow, Randall, now that I've seen your face. I ain't going to make you any richer by killing me. You can kill me and my missus for the small change in my pants pockets or you can leave now by the way you came in."

Frank Randall raised his gun to pistol-whip him again, but one of the others stopped him by saying, "You'll knock him cold and we'll have to wait for him to come to. Put away the gun. Use your fists on him like you did on her, but not on his head."

Randall holstered his gun and walloped Peppard a straight

right in the gut. The storekeeper doubled up in his nightshirt, wheezing and gasping.

"Now, I'm going to tell you something, Peppard," Frank Randall snarled at him, "and you listen real careful. It's been only a half day since my brother Jack was shot and killed. More than three hundred head of our cattle was drove into the mountains and lost. Gonzalez and his scum bandidos done it—yeah, that's right, the same one who buys all his hardware from you while you yes-señor him this, yes-señor him that. You ain't said yessir to none of us Randalls, only get yer ass out of my store if you can't pay cash, that's all we've ever had from you. Well, now you see why we've decided on you. We're low on cash, and you got plenty in that big safe of yours. Open it."

"You can shoot me sooner just as well as later," Peppard defied him.

"Damn you, I will too if you don't open that safe." Frank Randall drew his revolver and cocked it.

"Easy there," one of the other men said. "Look what I found in the old boy's coat pocket, hanging behind the door." He held up a brass key.

"See if it works," Frank rasped, keeping his gun barrel pointed at the storekeeper's head. "The safe's in back of the store, behind the counter, with a kind of drape hung down in front of it."

The one with the key lit another lamp and went out the door with it. In a few minutes they heard him shout, "It works! I got it open!"

Frank nodded to the other two men, and they went out of the bedroom, carrying the empty canvas bags they had brought with them. The storekeepere's wife began stirring and mumbling on the floor, where Frank's blow had put her. Frank said to Peppard, "Keep her quiet or she's as good as dead."

The storekeeper sat on the floor next to his wife, gently lifted her head onto his lap, spoke soothing words to her, and stroked her cheek.

When one of Randall's pards appeared in the bedroom doorway and held up a canvas bag that now seemed heavy to raise, Frank told him, "You boys go outside and hold my horse for me. I'll be with you in a minute." Then Frank turned to the storekeeper and his wife.

Peppard was looking at him defiantly, still cradling his semiconscious wife's head in his lap.

Randall said, "Pity she pulled down the bandanna on my face. I hadn't planned to do this, but now I got no choice."

He pointed the revolver almost point-blank at Peppard's forehead and squeezed the trigger.

Marshal Ben Stanton nearly fell out of his chair in his office when he heard the shot. If he wasn't quite sure what it was that woke him, the second shot a few moments later made things pretty clear for him. Before even taking his boots off the desk and heaving himself up out of his chair, he could tell that these were two revolver shots, fired inside a building, which had shattered Hachita's nocturnal silence. The marshal was used to all kinds of shots fired in the town limits, both in fun and in anger, and he noted a sinister, deliberate strangeness to these shots fired with a calm space between them. Somehow it was as if the shooter had been unhurried and careful.

The marshal grabbed his Winchester seventeen-shot repeating rifle as he went out his office door into the plaza. He saw the lighted windows at Peppard's hardware store and the men on horseback pulling away from outside it. He dropped to one knee, simultaneously levering a shell into the rifle's chamber, and blasted cartridge after cartridge after the shadowy horsemen as they galloped off into the surrounding darkness.

He went at a run to the hardware store and found Peppard and his wife shot through their foreheads in a back room.

A local man had followed him in. Stanton pointed to the powder burns on the skin around the entry wounds and said, "Bastard shot them at point-blank range in cold blood. They must have recognized him."

"Which means we know him too," the townsman said.

Stanton nodded. "Pity to see sweet folk go under in this way. I know a hundred people in this town I'd be pleased to see this happen to. Not this pair. We're gonna miss them."

In a little time the marshal and others discovered the empty safe and the ripped-off door hinges. What had happened was plain—the only question was who had done it.

"I saw four riders," the marshal claimed. "Now, that gives us a lot of choice as to who it could be."

That was the problem. It wasn't as if there were only a few drifters and badmen in town who could reasonably fall under suspicion—there were whole hordes of them. And some of these desperadoes were making sure they were being seen here in town at this hour, along with everyone else who had come out to see what was going on. The marshal appreciated their cooperation and nodded in recognition toward some of the men with the worst reputations, acknowledging that this was one they couldn't be accused of. The marshal observed that the big gunfighter who called himself Raider was present, and also the quack Weatherbee who was with Cynthia and for once in his life was not wearing his gray derby. With a practiced eye, the marshal combed through the gathered onlookers, looking for who was not there more than for who was. He sent his deputies and other townsmen to search for some men suspect by their absence. These were all quickly found, without exception, and were made so agreeable at the news they were now no longer suspects in the Peppards' murder, they didn't take any potshots at those who had disturbed them.

That left those who lived outside the town. With these, the possibilities were greatly narrowed down.

"It's either Gonzalez or the Randalls," one man opined, and there was a murmur of general agreement to this.

"Lobo and his crowd is friendly with Greg Peppard. Has been for years. Gonzalez is a crazy son of a bitch when you cross him. Rest of 'em out there with him are crazy too. But it's not like them to do this unless Peppard had given them some cause to do it. And I ain't heard of nothing like that happening."

A deputy named Morales said, "They were all good friends day before yesterday, when I last seen them together. Some of that money and gold dust stole from the safe belonged to Lobo. That's how much he trusted Greg Peppard. But you know who I heard was seen outside town earlier? Just a rumor, nothing certain. El Mellado. You think he might have done it?"

The marshal shook his head. "No way. He's fat and low slung and awkward, as well as being loco. I didn't see any of these four well enough to recognize them, but they were all of light build and medium height."

"Sounds like the Randalls for sure," another man said.

"Could be," Stanton allowed, "but not for sure."

"Thing we should do is git ourselves a posse and go after them boys," one man suggested—and almost immediately thought better of his suggestion. "Though still and all, we gotta think about what them Randalls did to the cowpunchers who rode into town to get back their stock."

The killing of these cowhands, which newspapers had reported throughout the territory, reports now being picked up by big eastern papers, was a sore point with the marshal. Way he saw it, there was nothing he could have done. If the Randall brothers could chase two dozen cowhands out of town, killing half of them in the process, how was he going to bring them under control? Besides, it had been a fair fight started by the cowhands. The Randalls had only been defending themselves and what they said was their property, which was only the God-given right of any citizen. The marshal had no objection to the U.S. Army coming to Hachita "to restore order," as so many of these newspapers demanded. Order had already been restored—the moment the cowhands quit tangling with the Randalls. The two-bit journalists claimed that since the battle had taken place inside the town limits, it was the marshal's responsibility to arrest "the perpetrators of this mass murder." Thing they couldn't seem to understand was that he, Ben Stanton, wasn't a marshal in the sense of being a marshal of Dodge City or some other boom cowtown. He wasn't appointed by the mayor. He wasn't elected by the people. Truth was, he was hired by the saloon owners to keep order in their establishments for the salary of $50 a month and all the free drinks he could consume. They wanted him to protect their gaming tables, not their customers. They knew he would lose his $50 salary back to them at their tables, which he did most months. When he couldn't pay for a room, he had to sleep in the marshal's office. Apart from protecting the gaming tables, any law enforcement that he did was strictly his own decision, out of the goodness of his heart, so to speak. Ben Stanton had liked Greg Peppard and his wife, but he wasn't so completely broke up that he was going to rush out like someone loco to attack the Randall brothers as their killers.

"We don't know for sure the Randalls done it," Stanton told the assembled men, "and there ain't much we can do about it in the middle of the night, seeing as how those old cabins they took over is all of eight miles from here at the very least. I say you all go back and have a big breakfast, take your time cleaning your guns and saddling up your horses. By then it should be sunup and we can all take a ride out there."

Stanton knew he could not avoid some kind of confrontation this time. He was hoping to go along as just one of the crowd, since whatever authority he had as marshal did not apply outside the town limits. Out by the Randall cabins, he would be just another citizen. Let whoever felt he could do so be the one to bring the Randalls to justice. Ben Stanton privately vowed it would not be he. Yet when the townsmen gathered with their horses at daybreak, it was plain that they looked to him as their leader.

They could expect no help from the sheriff of Grant County because Hachita was at the lower tip of the mountainous southern spur of that county, distant and cut off. Also, a sheriff's deputy had been slain in the town two years before in a tax dispute, and none of the residents had paid county taxes since that time.

Almost forty men rode out of town. Ben Stanton found himself reluctantly at their head. The mood of the men was subdued but determined. They were afraid of the Randalls — most of them had seen what had happened to the cowhands who had ridden into town confident of their large number. But they had all liked Peppard and his wife, and they knew they had to make a stand. Up until now the five brothers seemed untouchable, invincible. But Lobo and his men had killed one of them, and now there were only four brothers. The townsmen figured that the brothers themselves had to be shaken by Jack Randall's killing and the loss of their cattle — otherwise why would they stoop to such a brutal and stupid crime? As comancheros, the Randalls had been doing well, though it was rumored that they had to dispose of much stock at a loss during the time it was thought the U.S. Cavalry was on the way after the deaths of the cowhands. No one knew how much cash and gold and other valuables they had taken from Peppard's safe. The storekeeper kept his accounts in his head, and they had died with him.

When they had killed the cowhands, the Randalls had killed outsiders. This time they had killed one of the longest-established merchants in Hachita. If they were allowed to get away with this, no one in Hachita would be safe from them the next time they needed money or simply felt in a bad temper. Some few of the men thought to mention from time to time that they couldn't be sure the Randalls had done the killing. But all of them felt that the Randalls indeed had, and moreover all were fairly sure that no discussions would be necessary on this point—as soon as the Randalls saw them coming, they would start shooting. What would happen then, no one knew.

About two miles before the deserted miners' cabins that the Randalls had taken over at the base of the mountains, they saw three horsemen approaching. The horsemen appeared for a moment to be making a bolt for it, but they had no chance to do so because the townsmen rode up on them very fast. There were dozens of metallic scrapes and clicks as shells were levered in rifles and hammers thumbed back in revolvers. If any of the three horsemen had tried to ride off, his body would have picked up a pound or two in weight from the amount of lead it was carrying.

"Joe Randall," the marshal addressed the middle one of the three men, "what takes you out so early with a hurt arm?"

"I fell off my horse, Stanton, and broke a bone. I'm going to catch the stage out of Hachita where it passes on the trail down here and have my arm fixed in Deming."

"In Deming? Why not Hachita? We got a perfectly good doctor there. Plus that traveling physician who's now in town. Why go all the way to Deming?"

"Because it's a free country, Stanton, and I'll go where I like."

"Seems to me," the marshal went on, "like you might have a good reason to want to keep out of Hachita. I bet you boys was never expecting to meet us on the trail here, and you thought it would be easy for you to jump on that stage without ever coming into town. Thought we'd be afraid to come out here after you and your brothers, didn't you?"

Joe Randall said nothing, only glowered in silence at the marshal and the townsfolk. Like his brothers, he was small and fine-boned, sharp-featured, with bright blue eyes. His shirt and coat had their left sleeves cut off at the shoulder seams to allow a thick wadding of bandages to be wrapped from shoulder to wrist on the hurt arm. Blood had soaked through the bandages above the elbow and was now dried to a dark brown color.

"Maybe we can give you some medical advice," Stanton said, forgetting completely now his earlier resolution not to be the leader, to fade in among the crowd. He took out a bowie and, while the others covered Randall and his two companions, cut the bandages at Randall's wrists and unwound them. Both men were still on horseback, and with their horses' stepping around, Stanton's movements were none too gentle. Randall's face went deathly white, and his face contorted from the pain the marshal's handling of his arm was causing him. But he didn't make a sound.

The blood that stained the bandages above his elbow came from a bullet wound toward the front of his arm. He had another smaller bullet wound high on the back of his arm, near the shoulder.

Stanton looked at the arm for a moment longer. "He has two wounds, but I'd lay my life on it they were both caused by the one bullet. The bullet went in up here in the back of his arm, through the smaller hole, traveled down through his upper arm, smashing the bone as it went, and then exited here above the elbow, through the larger hole. I told you all how I emptied my Winchester repeater after the four men outside Peppard's store as they rode away. This man was hit from behind. Seems like not all my shots missed, like I thought they had."

Stanton pulled the pistol out of Joe Randall's holster and let it fall to the ground. This action functioned as a passing of judgment for the crowd. All three men were pulled from their horses. Two had their wrists bound behind their backs, while Joe Randall had his right hand bound to his belt and his injured left arm was let hang free. A stunted juniper stood nearby, the only tree of any size in sight.

One man stood beneath a thick overhanging branch, reached up, and touched it. "It'll only take their heels a few inches off the ground, but I reckon that'll be as good as a ten-foot drop." He laughed.

Several men began tying short lengths of rope to the branch and knotting nooses on their dangling ends. Joe Randall and one man walked quietly over to the tree, not letting anyone see fear showing on their faces. The third man shouted and struggled.

"Don't hang me! Not that! Please! I can tell you stuff you want to know!"

Ben Stanton stopped the men from dragging him toward the tree. "What can you tell us?"

"Promise first not to hang me. I wasn't there last night, at the hardware store."

"We won't hang you," the marshal promised, "if you tell us who was there and who shot Peppard and his wife."

"Those two were there," he said, indicating Joe Randall

and the other man. "It wasn't neither of them who killed the pair. Frank Randall and another man was along. It was Frank who shot them."

The marshall walked over to the tree and looked the two men in the eyes. "You heard that. What have you got to say for yourselves?"

"He's a lying skunk," Randall's man said.

Joe Randall himself said nothing, looking back at the marshal with cold unblinking blue eyes.

Stanton nodded toward Randall's gunslinger. A man at each side lifted him up off the ground by the elbows. A third man behind him placed a noose around his neck and tightened it. The men holding him by the elbows nodded to each other, raised him a little, and let him drop. Only then did the man start to struggle. All this time he had been looking straight in front of him with a rigid expression on his face. Now his mouth twisted open and he kicked wildly on the end of the rope. It wasn't a pretty sight as he slowly strangled to death. The sudden drop when the trapdoor on a gallows is opened usually snaps a man's neck when the weight of his falling body tautens the rope, and death is instantaneous. The way this man was dying was slow and painful. Every man there looked from his face to Joe Randall's face. Randall looked on like all this had nothing to do with him.

Three men took Randall by the knees and his good arm, while a fourth put the noose around his neck. Then they dropped him and watched him dance on the end of the rope.

"Joe!" one man shouted to him. "Your left arm ain't tied. All you got to do is raise it to free yourself."

That was plainly what Randall was trying to do, but he could get it out in front of him only a few inches before it hung lifelessly down from above the elbow. He died an ugly slow death.

This brought satisfaction to some in the crowd, self-disgust to others. Some started to kick and drag the third man toward the tree.

"Marshal, I wasn't there!" the man yelled in desperation. "You promised you wouldn't hang me!"

"Sure enough I did." The marshal stopped the men dragging him and they dropped the bound man on the ground. Stanton drew out his Colt .45 and angled the barrel down at the man's head. "Everyone hates a squealer," he said and squeezed the trigger.

The bullet shattered the cowering man's skull and scattered the white matter of his brain over the dusty ground and onto the riding boots of the townsman standing closest by.

"Reckon that finishes that," the marshal said. "Now we can go back to town."

No one suggested that they ride on farther and look for Frank Randall.

Tom and Clem had come over out of Texas and were experienced ranch hands who thought nothing of riding all day in the hot sun with only a water bottle and a plug of chaw tobacco to keep them going. No one knew anything else about them, including what their last names might be. They had ridden for the Lazy K for nearly six months, which almost qualified them as old-timers, and raised the question in some folk's minds that maybe there was some good reason for them to be lying low for so long down here under the Big Hatchet Mountains. Big Pete Caloway, owner of the Lazy K, regarded all such questions as invasions of a man's privacy. Anyway no one ever asked these kinds of questions directly, since most people who chose to live in and around Hachita had their own private reasons for being there and might not care to be questioned themselves.

Tom and Clem had seen a pair of real purty gals a couple of times down Eagle Pass way, when they were hunting for strays beyond the boundaries of the Lazy K. They happened to be over this way again, taking a ride off the ranch to see what they could find, something they did from time to time when they got bored. It so happened it was around midday, with the sun right in the middle of its arc, and they were feeling a little hungry. Maybe someone would offer to feed them salt pork and beans along with a mug of coffee if they happened by and food was on the table. They now knew that the two girls were the daughters of Harry Johnson, a small rancher and a drover, and that they lived in a pine-log ranch house at the side of a wooded hill. Good a place as any for pork and beans.

The two girls and their mother were in the kitchen of the house, and delicious smells of cooking came out the doorway where the two men stood.

"We were chasing down some strays, ma'am, and just happened by this way, over from the Lazy K spread. My name's Tom, this is Clem. We wondered if you could fill our water bottles."

The woman took the two bottles and went back inside, leaving the men standing outside the door. They heard her talking with her two daughters, then heard one of the girls giggling and the other ask her mother something in a pleading voice. Tom nodded to Clem, pushed in the door, and stepped inside.

"Who asked you in here?" the mother shouted in an alarmed voice.

"We just came in ourselves, ma'am, cause of the nice smell of cooking." Tom looked at the two girls. "Let me guess which one of you it was who done the cooking."

"It wasn't us, it was our mother," one girl said.

Tom turned to the older woman. "Then let me compliment you on it, ma'am. It smells the best I've come across since my mother's when I left home in Texas four years ago."

The woman looked at him sternly, but they could all see that she was pleased at his compliment. "It's only a beef stew—nothing special about it, not nearly as good as the one I make for particular occasions. Now sit you down, you two, and I'll serve you a bowl of it to fill you up. Put your guns on the hall stand by the door—it's my husband's rule no man sits at our table with a gun on his hip."

The two cowhands did as they were bidden and hungrily ate two helpings of stew each. Feeling in a playful mood on their full bellies, they drank coffee and flirted with the girls. The two girls, in their late teens, didn't see many young men this far out of town, and they made the most of the attention paid to them—to their mother's annoyance, since she felt her daughters were too good for these no-account Texas ranch hands. Things got out of hand when Tom demanded that one girl dance with him to a tune Clem whistled. The girl refused, she and her sister realizing that they had perhaps already encouraged the men too much.

"I ain't going to sit back down lest I get that dance," Tom said. "Maybe I'll settle for a glass of whiskey."

The girls' mother fetched a bottle and poured each of the men a quarter glass of the amber fluid. "Now drink that up and get you gone outta here," she said in a voice that clearly meant she would stand for no more nonsense.

Tom tried to grab the whiskey bottle out of her hand but missed. He jumped up and chased her round the table, while the two girls looked on, now mute and terrified. Clem stayed sitting at the table, laughing and sipping from his glass. Neither man noticed the door open or saw Harry Johnson step into his kitchen, an old Navy Colt in his right hand with the hammer cocked. By this time Tom had quit chasing the woman and had placed his arm around the girl who had refused to dance with him. Tom had his back to the door, and Harry Johnson closed the distance between them in a few quick steps and booted the cowman in the ass. Tom let go of the girl and swung about, his hand instinctively going to his right hip for his gun, which was no longer there but on the hall stand near the door. Clem had turned about now in his chair, and both men saw that Johnson stood between them and their guns. The big Navy Colt in his right hand looked just about ready to go off at any moment, and it kept pointing at their heads, first one's and then the other's.

"Time to hit the trail," Tom said to Clem, slow and easy.

"Reckon so," Clem agreed and unhurriedly got to his feet.

When they went toward their revolvers on the hall stand, Harry Johnson barked, "Reach another inch and I shoot."

The two men went out the door without their weapons, Tom pausing to look back and wink to the girl he had put his arm around.

Johnson went to a window to look out after them. "I saw their horses outside as I was coming back, and I don't know what tipped me off something was wrong. I took their rifles from their saddles and hid them in the long grass. I'll bring their guns into town later today and give them to Pete Caloway. He'll be at that town meeting on water rights."

Doc Weatherbee had persuaded Raider not to join the crowd of men who had ridden out at sunup to confront the Randalls over the murder of the storekeeper and his wife. Raider had been damn mad at the time and had wanted to go, but Doc's wisdom prevailed. They were both staying on in town, waiting for new assignments after the Double D case had fizzled out. If Tad Phillips chose to ask Lobo Gonzalez for help instead of the Pinkerton National Detective Agency, that was his decision and one they would respect. Neither of them would complain to headquarters, and thus indirectly to Phillips's aunt, the ranch's owner, that Tad had refused their offer of help. They were ready to move on. But the chances were, if anything reasonably big came up in the New Mexico Territory, they would end up together on it. Which didn't do much to make them any more tolerant of each other, stuck in a small mountain town in the back of beyond with nothing to do.

Of course there were always women, gambling, and drinking. And fighting. But they were only sidelines for Raider—he liked to have a case to work on at the same time, although he always looked forward to idleness when he was working. Doc was comfortable in cities and out of place in a small rough town like Hachita, yet he complained less and found more to occupy himself with than Raider.

Raider was pleased he hadn't gone along when the crowd of townsmen led by the marshal came back and told how they had hung Joe Randall and another man and how the marshal had shot a third. Raider would have enjoyed a shoot-out with the Randalls and a chance to avenge the Peppards' deaths in this way, but he wanted no part in a mob that was stringing people up, guilty or innocent. This had nothing to do with his being a Pinkerton—and his being a Pinkerton of course had been Weatherbee's main argument against his going. Raider liked to confront wrongdoers man to man and beat them on their own terms. Mobs and even towns, let alone cities, roused only distrust in him. He wouldn't even have thought of going if he hadn't been bored from doing nothing.

Doc was playing low-stakes faro in the Cottonwood Inn, and Raider was talking at the bar to cattlemen, miners, and others with vaguer means of support. One part of the saloon's interior had been roped off for a meeting that was to take place presently—an annual argument the local ranchers held about water rights in the forthcoming dry season. Those downstream told those upstream what they would do to them if they used more than their fair share. That was how the meeting went every year. The ranchers were already drifting in to have a few drinks beforehand so they could warm up for the event. Big Pete Caloway was at the end of the bar nearest the door. When Harry Johnson came in, he placed two rifles and two revolvers on the bar counter in front of Caloway.

"Couple of your young fellas got out of hand in my kitchen earlier today," Johnson told Caloway.

Caloway nodded. "They came back and told me what happened—your wife and daughters invited them in and they was all having a fine old time with food, whiskey, and dancing until you got home unexpected."

Men in earshot along the bar laughed at this.

"You're a damn liar, Caloway! My womenfolk wanted nothing to do with that trash. They shouldered their way in the door and forced themselves on helpless females. No real man does that. You know it. I know it."

"Nobody calls me a liar," Big Pete said, drawing himself up to his full height before the much smaller Harry Johnson.

"That was said in the heat of the moment, and I apologize for it," Johnson said. "This thing is no fault of yours. You had no way of knowing what your men were doing. It'd be a nice neighborly thing for you to pay off those two so's my womenfolk don't have to go on worrying maybe they will show up sometime again."

Caloway relaxed and laughed harshly. "Them women of yours might be just looking forward to seeing those two fine lads again. Course they can't tell you that. They gotta act annoyed in front of you. What I hear, when your back's turned it's a might different story."

"You may not be a liar, Caloway, but you sure are low scum." Harry Johnson's face was pale with rage, his eyes blazed, and his lips trembled.

"I already heard one apology from you," Pete said, real slow and easy. "Reckon I got a right to expect to hear another one coming up real fast."

"You're a low scum when you talk of my wife and daughters like you do."

Customers along the bar started paying serious attention and removing themselves a few steps away from these two.

Caloway spoke deliberately and slowly. "First you apologize to me for calling me that, and when you're done apologizing to me for that, then you apologize to Tom and Clem so I can pass it on to them." As he spoke, he tensed up to his full height and his right hand floated not too far off the handle of his Peacemaker.

"Low scum," was all Harry Johnson said.

"You'd better draw that old Navy Colt you got strapped on," Caloway said. "I'm waiting on you."

"I ain't about to draw," Johnson said, still raging but beginning to see clearly now what he had gotten himself into. "I got a family to keep. That's what I have to do, not match guns with the likes of you and maybe die on a barroom floor."

"You ain't got no choice, Johnson."

"Sure he has," a voice came from behind Caloway.

Big Pete whirled around. He saw the big man named Raider grinning at him up along the bar. Although this fella seemed slouched carelessly against the counter, Caloway wasn't fooled. It was an old gunfighter's trick pose.

"Stay out of what don't concern you," Big Pete told Raider.

"It concerns me."

"How?"

"That man's got a choice. He don't want to fight you. And he ain't gonna have to if he comes along here and has a drink with me."

Harry Johnson lost no time in scooting over behind Raider.

"Let it be," Big Pete said and went back to his drink.

• • •

That evening Doc Weatherbee stopped by the marshal's office for a chat.

"Don't see you selling, Doc. That wagon of yours been laying down in the stables gathering dust. You must be making money with your gambling."

"A little."

"Dang, I wish I could. I'd get rid of this tin star in a hurry, I tell you. This law-enforcement business is fun at first, but then it gets to wear you down."

"You expecting trouble?" Doc asked.

"Ain't you? Them Randalls will be coming in, shoot the town up, like as not, for us hanging Joe. Then they're on the warpath too against Lobo Gonzalez for killing their brother Jack. I tell you I'd breathe easier seeing the last of them. If they come into town raising hell, me and a lot of others will be waiting on them. They ain't wanted in Hachita anymore. Problem is, how do you make them understand that? Them Randalls are kinda slow to hear anything they don't want to know."

"Can't you slap some charge on them or find if they're wanted back in Texas?"

Ben Stanton pushed a heavy book across his desk to Doc. "How many pages does it have?"

Doc opened the book to its last page and read the page number. "Two hundred twenty-six."

"Now look at the book. There are 4,402 fugitives listed in it, many of them wanted for murder, and they're all from Texas. That whole book is just Texas fugitives from justice. Other places, they have wanted posters. Texas, they have to have a big book. And any man on the dodge from the Texas law can feel reasonably safe once he crosses the line into New Mexico."

Doc was leafing through the book in amazement. "I didn't think things had gotten this bad down here."

"They have."

Stanton brought out a bottle of Taos lightning. Doc usually tried to avoid this popular rotgut, distilled in Taos, because of its strength and physically damaging effects, but he accepted a glass so as not to offend the marshal.

"My big hope," Stanton went on, "is that them Randalls will have a big shoot-out with the Gonzalez bunch and will get themselves cremated. You don't see too much of Gonzalez and his men here in town, but that don't mean they're not around. After you been here awhile, you get to seeing there's really two towns here, the Anglo one and the Spanish one. One don't pay much attention to the other until someone steps on someone's toes. We all go to the same stores and the same saloons, and things is peaceful enough between us, but that's only because we keep it that way. A lot of Anglos here would be surprised to learn that Lobo Gonzalez more or less runs this town, though a month could pass and you wouldn't see him in it. However, you make the mistake of crossing the Gonzalez bunch and there ain't no place you're gonna be safe around here. Them Randalls is too stupid to see that. Now they stole Gonzalez's money from that safe, and Lobo and his bandidos will be looking for them. That could solve all our problems for us."

"I hope so," Doc said.

"Or it could make things worse. They could burn down the town between them." The marshal yawned, settled himself in his chair, and stretched his legs on the desk top. "Been up since the Peppard trouble started—the shots woke me—and I haven't had a chance to take a nap since. Now that it's past sundown, I reckon things will be quiet."

Perhaps fearing there would be trouble, the usual customers at the saloons stayed away and most places closed early. The plaza was almost deserted shortly after ten o'clock, when a horseman rode into town. The stars showed in a clear sky, and by their light and the glow of lamps in occasional windows, the rider picked his way carefully along. He passed a lighted window and looked in, his sharp features and bright blue eyes illuminated clearly for a moment but unseen by the man sleeping on the office chair inside. The horse's hooves made a light thudding in the dust, which was not enough to wake the sleeping man. In a moment the rider and horse had passed on and out of the light projected from the window.

In the dark once more, Frank Randall drew out his American Arms double-barrel 12-gauge shotgun. He pulled back both hammers and turned his horse around, to walk past the window again. This time, when the horse walked into the lamplight from the window, the rider had the short-barrel shotgun to his shoulder. He aimed for the head of the sleeping marshal and gave him a left and a right.

The first blast shattered the glass from the window and carried through to pepper the upper part of Ben Stanton's body. The second blast had nothing to deflect it, and the shot particles ripped through the marshal's flesh and broke open his skull without dislodging him from his chair.

Frank Randall paused a moment to make sure his aim had been true, then gave his horse its head and galloped off out of the plaza into the night as the glow of oil lamps being lit showed in the houses.

CHAPTER SEVEN

Ben Stanton's body, covered with a horse blanket to hide his head and shoulders, which had been mutilated by the shotgun blasts, still lay on the floor of the marshal's office at eight the next morning, when two hundred head of cattle were driven through the plaza by the remaining three Randall brothers and their men. The brothers and their eleven men ran the animals into the pens at the far end of town.

"The marshal deserves better than this," one man said.

"If Lobo Gonzalez lived in town, they wouldn't try this," another said.

"Big Pete Caloway would put a stop to it too, 'cept he's out on the Lazy K."

Despite the mutterings, no one did anything. Doc Weatherbee insisted on buying Raider a big breakfast in an eating house so he could keep an eye on him and make sure he didn't get involved. Buyers came in from out of town, and the Randalls got back to business in a big way. It was said they

had bought the two-hundred cattle they drove into town with
some of the cash they had stolen from Peppard's safe. Ani
mals bought with blood money, the buyers were warned
could bring them only bad luck. But men who dealt with
comancheros like the Randalls were not easily put off by
superstitions like that.

Their business done, cattle sold and bought, the Randall
and their gunslicks walked through the plaza on their way to
the Cottonwood Inn. They showed the townfolk they had no
need for horses here—this was their town, and they couldn'
be hurried in it. Frank and his brothers passed the marshal's
office without glancing in through the window, empty but for
a few shards of glass still stuck in the frames. This insult was
too much for one man. He called down Frank Randall while
he was still a hundred paces off and drew his revolver. Frank
pulled his Colt Peacemaker out of its holster and kept walking. His brothers and the other men stayed where they were.

"It's Morales," a townsman said. "He's crazy to go
against Frank Randall alone."

"The others are staying back. It's a fair fight."

The two men walked toward one another, their revolvers
drawn but hanging by their sides. Morales had shouted only
his opponent's name. Nothing else. There was no need for
insults or harsh names. Everyone knew, Frank Randall
included, that Angel Morales was a deputy marshal, and
word was out that Frank had killed Marshal Ben Stanton.
Morales was also known to be Lobo Gonzalez's man in the
marshal's office. No one believed that Lobo had ordered him
to do something like this. What Morales was doing now was
what many a man there would have liked to do, but didn't
have the nerve to do.

About sixty paces now separated the two men. They were
looking in each other's faces, walking with a steady gait,
neither showing any sign of doubt or weakness.

At fifty paces, without halting, Angel Morales raised his revolver and fired. The shot went over Frank Randall's head. Randall just kept walking. Morales fired again. This time the bullet sped past Randall's left shoulder, so close he could feel the wind from it on his neck.

Morales stopped at forty paces, pausing to raise the revolver to the level of his eye and take careful aim. Randall quit his walk too, whipped his Colt .45 up, and squeezed off a shot.

The bullet caught Morales in the gut, and he bent double and moved his body from side to side with a loud moaning hum. Randall fired again and hit him in the shoulder, straightening his body up, then blasted two more slugs into him, which spun him around and flopped him in the dust.

Others ran to aid the fallen man. Frank Randall ejected the empty cartridges and fitted fresh ones in the chambers as he waited for his brothers and their men to come up to him, smile, and slap him on the back.

The eating house didn't serve beer at breakfast. This alone would have been enough to annoy Raider, but for him to have to put up with Weatherbee's yapping this early in the day along with not having the essentials of a decent breakfast was doing nothing to put him in a good mood. They stood up from the table and went outside when they heard the shooting. Both were upset, since they had liked Morales, and they returned to their table to sip coffee moodily.

"It gives me a pain in the gut to have to sit quiet and let louses like them Randalls rule this town," Raider growled to nobody in particular. He thought about this for a while and brightened a little when he said, "Mebbe one of them will pick a fight with me."

Doc looked at him judgmentally. "Make sure *he* picks it, not you. And I don't have to remind you, you will be alone.

Under no circumstances will I become embroiled in these small-town shenanigans."

Raider scowled when he saw who was coming in the door of the eating house—Tad Phillips. When Phillips came toward their table, Raider shoved back his chair and got ready to leave.

"You got a right to be annoyed with me, Raider," Tad said, "but don't leave yet till you hear this. I know you two think bad of me for getting Lobo's help instead of yours— and I guess too you don't think of me as your typical rancher who likes nothing better than to ride around on his horse fourteen hours a day and count cows. I'd prefer to sit in an armchair and read a newspaper. But I'm not the class A fool and layabout that you maybe think I am. I had to go to Lobo Gonzalez for help against the Randalls and turn down your offers. I had no choice. Lobo calls the shots out on the Double D, and I go along with what he says. Otherwise I wouldn't have lasted down here—I'd have been like all those who had tried to make a success of the Double D before and failed. If I brought in what he would consider outside help— you two—Lobo would have taken it as a combined insult and challenge to him. Can you see my position?"

"I could," Raider said, "if it was maybe ten at night and we was bellying up to a bar with a bottle of bourbon in front of us. At this hour of the morning, over the watery coffee they serve in this place, I gotta say I couldn't give a blind fuck about your position or what you feel you gotta do on the Double D. Talk to Weatherbee here. He likes to talk shit. I have to leave."

Tad laughed. "Hold it, Raider. I changed my mind. I need Pinkerton help. Is that straightforward and plain enough for you?"

"It's a start," Raider allowed and sat back on his chair again.

"You saw what just happened outside in the plaza?" Tad went on. "Angel Morales was a decent, honest man. By local standards, so too was Ben Stanton. Greg Peppard and his wife were certainly harmless people. Now, no one cares when gunslingers, bandidos, and comancheros meet their end, but when storekeepers and lawmen in a town—"

"What has this got to do with the Double D?" Raider asked impatiently. He wanted to make it clear to Phillips that he couldn't take Raider's help for granted and that Raider didn't have to sit and listen while Phillips bullshitted.

This time Tad Phillips was taken aback. "I'm nervous. It's making me ramble. First thing this morning, Pete Caloway and some men arrived at the Double D. I was already up, having an early morning billiard game, since I don't sleep good. Caloway said he had bought the ranch and gave me forty-eight hours to be off the property."

"Have you heard nothing from your aunt about this?" Doc asked.

"Nothing. But now I'm beginning to think that there might be more to her hiring you Pinkertons to check things out here than she first admitted to Allan Pinkerton. Maybe she had this sale to Caloway in mind all the time and needed Pinkerton operatives to check on what was really happening down here."

"Sounds reasonable," Doc had to admit. "And she would have no duty to report the ranch's sale to the agency, since officially we're off the case after I reported back that you didn't want our help. I said nothing about Lobo Gonzalez, of course. Well, you still have two days before you have to leave, and in that time I can telegraph our Chicago head-quarters and have their reply."

"Just before coming in here, I telegraphed Mrs. Phillips —I suppose I should say, my aunt—to ask her what was going on. What makes me really suspicious is that I'm sure

Caloway doesn't have the cash to buy the spread at a fair price."

"We'll soon find out," Doc said. "But we're going to have to wait for Chicago's reply and their authorization before we can take action."

Raider belched and said grumpily, "While Doc is taking care of the formalities, if Caloway edges in on you, I'll shoot his balls off with this Remington."

Tad Phillips smiled gratefully. "I'll tell him that."

Phil Conners, foreman at the Lazy K, came up to Raider in the Cottonwood Inn. "I saw you and that traveling doctor earlier on talking with Tad Phillips. Was he telling you about the visit my boss paid on him this morning?"

Raider looked him in the eye. "Why are you asking me that?"

Phil tried to sound casual. "I thought he might be hiring you as a gun. I don't know what he would want with that doctor fella—he don't look like no fighting man to me—unless it's to patch him up after Big Pete Caloway is finished with him."

"You worried me and you might end up on opposite sides in this, Phil?"

"I'm not sure I'd care to be around for that," Conners said readily. "I think you'd be a mean son of a bitch with a shooting iron."

"Then take care you're on the same side as me," Raider warned him, unsmiling. "We can always use an extra man."

"So that means you'll be working for Phillips?"

"I'm sure thinking along those lines," Raider told him. "So long as Caloway plays things legal, I ain't going to step in. But once he steps off that straight and narrow path, I'm going to lay him low."

"Caloway is going to get the Double D spread, one way or

another. If he can't buy it, he's gonna grab it."

"He got the money to buy the place?"

"No way," Phil said. "He's been trying to scare that widow woman back east into selling the spread to him dirt cheap because of the troubles down here. The fly in that ointment is that Tad Phillips is making the ranch pay—and you seen him, he ain't no proper cowman. Caloway figures he's paying off Lobo Gonzalez with steers so he don't rob him too much, which is a hell of an idea, because if Lobo and his boys put their minds to it, they could empty the place of beeves any time they wanted to and no one could stop them. Excepting hombres like you, of course." Phil grinned. "I heard you gunned down one of Lobo's men you caught stealing stock. What'd you do that for?"

"I was trying to persuade Phillips to give me a job hunting rustlers on bounty. He wouldn't, though. I expect he pays off Lobo, like you say. But if I work for him this time, I'll be watching Big Pete Caloway closer than I will Lobo Gonzalez. Were you with Caloway when he rode out to see Phillips?"

"No, but I knew all about it," Conners said. "I'm getting to feel I'm being a traitor to my boss. I ain't this disloyal usually, only now I see some ugly things straight ahead that I want no part of."

"You ain't being a traitor to no one so long as you choose up sides before the fight begins," Raider told him. "Sticking by someone you know is doing wrong ain't loyalty—that's being a damn fool, that's being a traitor to yourself."

But Phil Conners was no longer listening to him. He was staring at a man standing by the bar with a marshal's star on his shirt. "Ain't that Bob Holloway, one of the Randalls' gunslicks?" Phil asked Raider, although he himself knew the man, while the Pinkerton didn't. Phil was clearly having trouble believing what his eyes were telling him. "I'll be danged. Who made that goon a marshal?"

"I guess the Randalls are halfway to owning this town now," Raider suggested.

"They may think that," Phil replied, "but I know some folk who are going to have something to say about it. And one of them is Big Pete. He's going to start oiling up his guns when he hears that the Randalls must have scared the saloon owners into hiring one of their men as marshal after they killed the old one. And you can bet it was them that done it, even if no one got a look at that shotgun-toting sidewinder in the dark. I better ride out to the Lazy K with the news right away. Big Pete's going to grind his teeth when he hears this."

Frank Randall's blue eyes watchfully scanned the scrub-covered hills. There were no other riders in sight anywhere. "Looks good," he said to his brother Luke and four other men. He dug his heels into his horse's sides and yanked on the reins so the bit pulled painfully in the horse's mouth.

The six men spread into a crosswise line, riding abreast within a stone's throw of one another and gathering up the grazing longhorns as they went. As the cattle bunched up, two men went forward on each side to keep the building herd from breaking to either right or left, and the remaining two continued to drive the animals from behind. The men shouted and waved their arms and sometimes their hats to keep the cattle moving, yet they were slow and careful in maneuvering the beasts. Anytime the steers broke into a run, they pulled back and eased the pressure on them till they had calmed to a walk again. The one thing they wanted to avoid was making the steers nervous enough to stampede.

Frank reckoned they had about one hundred twenty head, and he yelled to two of the riders not to bother to try to round up another forty or so head grazing on the side of a hill they were passing. He knew how easy it was to lose a whole herd by being too greedy and not being happy with what you've got. A new bunch of animals driven into the herd could cause the newcomers and the others to spar among one another with their horns, get part of the herd acting crazy and wild, start the whole bunch running, break out of control of the six riders . . .

"Good heavy beeves," Frank said to his brother Luke as they rode behind the herd. "They'll fetch a nice price and be easy to sell fast. Be gone out of the town pens by midday tomorrow."

Luke nodded in agreement, running an expert eye over the fat cattle with the Double D brand prominent on one flank. The brand's second D was lower than the first, and the mark was easy to see in the hide and instantly recognizable from some distance. It wouldn't be hard to change to a Double P, but this was not the kind of work the Randalls bothered themselves with. There was a lot less labor and time spent in forging a piece of paper, such as a bill of sale, than in trying to rope and change the brands of grown and dangerous longhorns.

Besides the brand, each of the cattle had two triangular notches cut out of the lower edge of the left ear—another identifying mark that was easy to see. The two Randall brothers and their men had no way of knowing that these notches were how Tad Phillips and Lobo Gonzalez could tell Gonzalez cattle apart from regular Double D stock. The Gonzalez steers had the notches. And wherever there were Gonzalez cattle, there was a Gonzalez gun not too far distant.

"Ride up to the top of that hill and fire this rifle four times," Miguel Santiago told the rider with him. "It's our signal for trouble."

The man looked frightened and confused. "Me?" he said.

"You'd probably fuck it up," Santiago rasped. "I'll do it myself. You ride down and delay them."

"Delay them?"

"Shit, yes. Do something to earn your keep." Santiago whacked his horse and galloped off to fire the signal shots from the hill.

He's right, El Mellado thought as he rode toward the riders and cattle. I should do something for Lobo to show him gratitude for hiding me from the law and for listening patiently to me when I explain about the curse that was put on me.

What should he do? Lobo didn't allow him to carry a gun or a knife. He rode faster. He would think of something.

"Hey, who's this asshole riding into us?" Luke asked in alarm.

Frank was farsighted. "It's El Mellado."

Luke pulled his rifle from the saddle scabbard. "That dog killed his woman. I'll nail him—ain't no one going to charge me with that."

"Your shot will scare the cattle," Frank said urgently. "They're nervy and jumpy now. It ain't worth losing them for the fun of shooting that loco varmint."

"You're right," Luke agreed reluctantly and shoved his rifle back in its scabbard. "And he's on the run himself, so he won't be no witness against us for this."

"No one would believe him even if he tried."

El Mellado rode up to them without scaring any of the steers. "You hear about the curse that witch put on me?"

"Sure, we heard about the curse, Mellado," Frank said. "I hear you're hiding out with Lobo. How you like all that goddamn hot Mexican food they eat out there?"

"I like hot food," Mellado said seriously. He showed them his almost bare gums. "Mexican food is easier to chew as well."

The two Randalls cracked up at this and told each other this was about the funniest thing they'd heard in a long time.

Then, even though they said they already knew about it, he told them about the curse that had been placed on him. Mellado tried to gradually slow down, but the cattle had settled into a fixed pace, so slowing the riders did not slow them. While he was telling them about the curse, he desperately searched his mind for some way to delay them.

They heard four shots. The Randalls and their men threw anxious, puzzled looks among themselves.

"Keep 'em moving," Frank yelled. "I don't see nothing."

"They're waiting up ahead," Mellado said with the innocence of a child.

Frank looked at him. "What did you say?"

"That's the signal to Lobo. He's lying in wait for you. I don't know why they said I had to come down here and ride with you. I thought they were my friends."

"Holy fuck!" Frank gasped. "This is a trap. Them buzzards aim to bushwhack us." He called his four men back, and the cattle ran by themselves for a spell before stopping and breaking up. "Let's leave the Double D alone. The Lazy K is over here only a little ways, and we can visit there instead. So long, Mellado. You done us a service. Next time you come into the Cottonwood Inn, remind me to buy you a drink."

They hooted with laughter at that and rode away toward Caloway's spread. El Mellado felt proud to have outwitted them. Finally he was earning his keep. This made him feel good. If it only wasn't for the curse she had put on him and the trouble he was having shaking it off . . .

"She said she didn't sell the place and ain't going to sell it as long as I keep it a going concern." Tad Phillips showed Doc and Raider the telegram he had received from the ranch's owner. "I guess she ain't such a bad dame after all."

Doc produced the telegram he had received from Pinker-

ton headquarters. He placed the handwritten message on
Western Union paper on the table so Tad could read it.

You and Raider are authorized to give all assistance to
subject. Client admitted to our associates that she had
been in negotiation with potential buyer you mentioned by name, but deal fell through because no serious offer was made and because of your favorable
report on the subject. Our associates remonstrated with
client for being less than frank with us and were
assured that nothing else is being concealed concerning this case. Client is sending subject separate notifi-
cation.

Wagner

"So the bitch *was* thinking of selling out," Tad murmured.

"Can you blame her?" Doc asked. "You can imagine the
things Caloway was probably telling her about you and about
what a rough town Hachita is. He was telling the truth about
Hachita, of course."

In a good mood, they remained sitting and talking at the
table in the Cottonwood Inn. After a time Big Pete Caloway,
Phil Conners, and other Lazy K men came into the saloon.
He and Conners came over in a little while and stood at their
table, looking down at Doc's telegram now stuck by a wet
corner to the table surface. Caloway rooted in an inside
pocket and pulled out his own telegram. He grinned at their
obvious surprise.

"Says you boys are Pinkertons," he told them jovially. "I
gotta say you had me fooled. But I can tell you this, it might
as well say you're British Redcoats for all the good being
Pinkertons will do you down here. Your Mr. Pinkerton may
be a big man in a lot of places, but in Hachita the name
Caloway means one hell of a lot more."

"Who sent you your telegram?" Doc inquired.

Caloway squinted at it. "Name here is Wagner. You can tell he's a snooty sort by the words he uses."

"He's a stuck up stupid bastard," Raider said. "He never even told us he was sending word to you."

"Well, he's telling me here that there's going to be no sale of the Double D," Big Pete went on. "Now, I want you boys to know that I'm going to get that land. We're just talking friendly now between ourselves. I ain't dumb. I don't want no trouble I can avoid. What I'm saying to you is this: you tell me what could persuade you to move on out and forget this."

"I'm staying," Tad said.

Doc said to Caloway, "If you think we would go for an offer like that, you don't know us Pinkertons."

"But you will," Raider added in a sinister tone.

"I don't scare easy, Raider," Big Pete said in an amused tone. "But I ain't in town to deal with you tonight. I been looking in the pens for cattle of mine that got stole off the Lazy K earlier on today. Them Randall hogs stole them, and you can bet that new marshal ain't gonna interfere. They're gonna turn this town into a rustlers' stockyard."

Just talking about the Randalls and his stolen cattle made him visibly enraged. He stomped off.

Before Phil Conners followed him, he said to Tad Phillips, "I'd be real careful from now on if I was you. Don't go anywhere alone."

"Since word will soon be around that we are Pinkertons," Doc said, "we're not going to learn very much by staying here in town. At least one of us should move out to the ranch with you, Tad."

"Meaning me," Raider said.

"Exactly," Doc agreed.

A man was shouting at the bar. "Lobo's calling down the marshal outside in the plaza!" There was a rush for the door.

When Raider and Doc made their way outside, they saw Gonzalez men on all sides of the plaza, armed with shotguns and rifles. These men were busy minding their own business, looking at their feet or at the ground, not threatening anybody. But they were obviously at the beck and call of Lobo, who was walking up and down outside the marshal's office, yelling for the new marshal to show himself. Bob Holloway was letting him wait, or else he wasn't inside.

Although many of Lobo's men were got out in fancy bandido style, with hand-tooled leather boots and gunbelts sporting crafted silver inlays and buckles, Lobo himself was turned out plain in an old blue flannel shirt, denims, and a battered hat—like any regular no-account cowhand instead of the leader of a private army, which in fact he was. And the townsfolk were appreciating the way he was putting himself on the line to avenge his friend, the slain deputy Angel Morales. Lobo was not hiding behind his triggermen. A thing like that was noted and approved in Hachita.

"Come out, you murdering swine," Lobo shouted. "My men out here ain't going to shoot you, 'cause they're leaving that to me. They're here to watch my back from any Randall coyotes that might be prowling around. If you get the better of me, they'll walk to their horses and ride out of town. You can believe what I say. People in Hachita know me as a man of my word. I ain't going to lose that reputation for a louse like you. You ain't worth it. Come on out and match me with your gun. Best man wins."

There was a long silence and no movement from the marshal's office.

Lobo laughed and shook his head as if at the foolishness of the new marshal. "Bob Holloway, I know you're in there, 'cause I've had men watching for you. They saw you go in, and no one's seen you leave. Now, when you took on the job as marshal of this here town, what did you expect? Did the

Randalls tell you they'd always be here to hold your hand? Is that what they told you? Is that what you believed? Did you think you was going to lord it over this town with your little tin star and nobody was going to stand up to you? Hell, no one is that dumb. But maybe you was. Listen, I'll make you an offer. You open that door and throw your star out here in the dirt, then leave your gunbelt behind and head down to the stables and clear out of town. I know you wasn't the one who shot Angel, and I ain't about to shoot an ex-marshal with no gun who's quit working for murdering scum. You coming out? With or without your gun, either way."

There was a long wait. Lobo was giving him time to think it over. But no sign came from the marshal's office.

"I ain't in no hurry, Holloway. I learned to be a patient man while living up in them hills looking down on the land stole from my family. I ain't about to rush you. You take your time and think real good. And I'll tell you something else I ain't concerned about—you playing for time. Maybe you think that if you delay long enough, your Randall buddies is going to ride in and rescue you. I hope they try it. That's what I brought all these men here for. We're going to chop 'em into vulture food. But they ain't such fools as that. They're not going to have their asses shot off to save a hired hand like you. Now—one of two things: you're either the marshal of this town or you ain't. You either come out and shoot or you throw out that star and hit the trail. Can't be no more simple than that."

The door of the marshal's office opened inward. Bob Holloway stood in the doorway. He was wearing his star and his gun.

"Well, lookit here," Lobo greeted him. "Here comes the law-enforcement officer bestowed on us through the courtesy of the three Randall brothers, who were once five and who soon will be none at all. You walk out here with that badge, Holloway, you're going to have to use that gun."

Bob Holloway said nothing but stepped forward. He was plainly having trouble keeping his fear under control, but he wasn't a coward, and this wasn't the first bit of gunplay he'd been invited to. He kept coming.

Lobo quieted down, and a wary look came over his face. It was one thing to shout threats at a closed door, and still another when the door opened and a man came out to face you. Lobo knew that Bob Holloway was a professional gunfighter and that he would be no easy man to take. Gonzalez had put Holloway's courage to the test and had been answered. Now it was time for him to show his own.

Raider watched with a cool detachment unusual for him as the two men squared off on the dusty, wheel-rutted plaza. Men moved out of the line of fire behind each of the adversaries. The two stood no more than fifteen paces apart. Holloway was acting the marshal, looking like he had the law behind him, not a man to be crossed. Gonzalez was playing his own game, making Holloway wait on him to draw, seeing if he could stir fear in him, making him shaky for a moment. That would be the moment when Lobo would go for his gun. But it wasn't all Lobo's show—he knew Holloway might reach at any moment himself without waiting for Gonzalez to draw first. They were sizing each other up, searching for an edge, showing each other who had the steadier nerve.

As Lobo had figured he might, Holloway slapped leather first, hoping to catch him by surprise or maybe just wanting to end it all, one way or the other. Bob's Colt .45 came up fast out of its holster, and as it came he thumbed back the hammer. He had a neat, clear-thinking way of pulling his gun, not a movement wasted, not a moment lost. When the barrel was level his forefinger hooked over the trigger and squeezed. . . .

Lobo drew like a horse kicked—evil, wicked, mean,

fast. There was nothing graceful or economical in his movements. He just hung on to the grips of his shooting iron,
dragged its barrel out of the holster, snapped the gun cocked
as it came, pointed it any old way in the general direction of
his opponent, and squeezed the shot off before he had the
barrel properly leveled. There was no way that kind of
shooting could beat the smooth actions of a professional
gunslinger. But it did. Lobo had the instincts of a born
fighter. His poorly aimed bullet caught Bob Holloway in the
lower belly, a few inches above the groin, as his forefinger
squeezed on the trigger.

As Lobo's .45-caliber lead bullet tore into his soft under-
belly, Holloway's aim went wide. His bullet passed inches to
the left of Lobo's forehead, and he wasn't taking any second
shot as the pain closed in on him and he dropped his gun so he
could clutch himself.

"Man should have rode out of town while he had the
chance," someone said to Raider.

"I dunno," the big Pinkerton replied. "I reckon I'd do
what Holloway done. I just wouldn't have taken so long
about it to make up my mind."

Doc Weatherbee lay on the bed beside Cynthia.

"You hear who the next marshal is going to be?" she asked
him.

"Miguel Santiago. One of the Gonzalez bunch."

"Until one of the Randalls gets him," Cynthia said with
disgust.

"Maybe."

"You sound as if you don't think he'll be any better than
the last one. I don't. How come you never told me you was a
Pinkerton?"

"You never asked."

She poked him in the ribs. "Maybe you're a U.S. senator,

too. Or the governor of Ohio. Do I have to ask everything?"
She answered her own question. "I guess I do."

"I'm thinking maybe I'll have to move out and stay on the
Double D spread," Doc volunteered. "Will you come
along?"

"No way."

"Too dull for you?"

She said, "I spent the first fifteen years of my life looking
at grass and tumbleweed stretching off in any direction I
cared to look. A few ornery beasts would pass by every now
and then, stir up some dust, chew on the grass. Maybe a
cloud would pass by in the sky—might remind me of the
shape of a Spanish galleon or something else I'd seen in a
picture book. There was nothing out there to see. Then one
day I just couldn't stand it no more. You're gonna have to gag
and hog-tie me before you get me on a ranch again."

"I'm not going to do that," Doc assured her.

"Pity," she said. "I mighta liked it."

Doc lightly placed his hand on her furry mound. She
dozed off under the comforting, pleasurable feel of his hand.
He let one finger slip between the lips of her sex. She stirred
but did not wake. He waited for her slumbering, vulnerable
flesh to accustom itself to his touch. He caressed her softly,
and her legs parted a bit more. His finger found her clit and
massaged it gently. She stirred again and said something in
her sleep that he couldn't understand. She was moist on his
finger now. Her lips were smiling; she was having a nice
dream.

Soon her hips started to move, and Doc slipped a second
finger in and slid them both into her vagina. She squirmed
and gasped beneath his hand now, clutching his arm, no
longer sleeping. She felt his cock erect against her side and
she clutched it in her hand.

"Gimme this!" she whined. "I want to feel this inside me."

Doc twisted her onto her stomach, lifted her so that her knees were bending and pressed her head and shoulders onto the bed in submission to him. He held on to the smooth cheeks of her ass and slowly pushed his ramrod into her cunt from behind. She yelped as he thrust the hot shaft deep inside her pussy.

He drove his cock into her long and hard, while she moaned with the unbearable pleasure of it. She reached beneath her and played with her clit to heighten the ecstasy his hard-driving member was giving her. Then with a series of steadily louder cries, she entered a climactic frenzy and struggled like a mad thing impaled on his cock.

As her manic passion and writhing and thrashing weakened, he felt his semen surge inside his cock and, in a wild jag of pleasure, burst loose to fill her insides.

CHAPTER EIGHT

Raider and Doc Weatherbee happened to be at the Double D ranch house when the Randalls arrived. Frank, Luke, and Bart left their horses at the drinking trough next to the barn, along with the five riders who had come with them.

Doc spoke as they came to the ranch house door. "Come in, gentlemen. We haven't seen any of you in town in a while. I thought you might have moved on to someplace new."

Frank led his brothers inside. "We ain't here to jaw with you, Weatherbee. We come to talk to Tad Phillips."

Doc was unperturbed by this show of unfriendliness. "Well, you see Tad right there in front of you, but it's my duty to warn you that, with Tad's consent, you won't be doing any negotiations with him unless my colleague Raider and I are involved. We Pinkertons have fixed ways of doing things, and I suggest that if you boys wish to get something done, you do it our way."

Frank looked at Doc in silence for a while. "You done spoutin'?"

Raider laughed heartily, happy to make Doc look a pompous fool.

"We come here to offer you a deal, Phillips," Frank Randall said. "We know you don't own this place, so we want you to pass the word on. Whatever Caloway offers you, we'll top it."

"Caloway ain't offered us shit, so topping his bid would be easy," Tad said. "Forget Caloway. You come up with a substantial offer and show how you're in a position to pay it, then the widow woman who owns this place might want to listen to you. I don't know. But I will pass on any serious offer you give me. You name the dollars and persuade me you got them—that's what I call a serious offer. I won't pass on any loose talk or threats. That's why we got these two Pinkertons down here, so they can listen to you boys when you want to talk tough."

"I think you missed my point, Tad," Frank said, smooth as swamp water. "I hear Caloway's been pushing hard on this widow woman to make a sale. Now, I think that's the right way to go about it, except I don't have a lawyer back east to pressure the widow woman like Big Pete has. So what I'm saying is not that we're going to bid on this ranch like it was nice safe property that you could hold on to if you didn't like the prices you was offered. No, that's not how my brothers and me see it at all. All we can do for you is give you a better offer than Caloway's. Not a way-to-hell-over-the-hills better offer than his. Just a plain better offer."

"No deal." Tad Phillips's voice was flat and determined.

"I've had men say that to me before," Frank said quietly, "and I've seen them change their minds."

"That's 'cause I wasn't there taking their part," Raider put in with a friendly grin.

Frank Randall looked at him. "I'm telling you plain and simple to stay out of this."

"You're wasting your time," Raider responded. "First thing I want to know is how much of the money you'll offer for the Double D came from the late Greg Peppard's safe."

Frank turned white with rage. "I can see we're getting nowhere with you Pinkertons here. Remember this, Phillips, we're going to take over the Double D, and we don't care what we have to do to get it."

"That's what Pete Caloway told me," Tad said.

"Caloway ain't nothing but mush," Frank growled. "It's us Randalls you gotta watch out for."

Tad grinned. "I'll tell Big Pete that."

"Clem, you see what I'm seeing?"

Clem looked in the direction Tom was pointing. Harry Johnson was cutting across the Lazy K land on his way into Hachita. Clem said, "It's him all right."

Johnson didn't see the two Lazy K cowhands sitting on their mounts on a scrubby hill above him. They watched him till he passed out of sight in the direction of town.

"I ain't even seen a woman since last payday," Tom said. "And I won't have no money for another week to buy me one. It's real tormenting to know there's two fine young ones just going a-wasting no more than an hour's ride from here."

"They're still only girls, Tom."

"Damn it, man, they're eighteen, nineteen—in the prime of their life. If they're too tender for you, take their mother. That bitch will sure lay it to you."

"But she'll tell her husband, the girls will tell their pa," Clem objected. "We ain't afraid of him, but he'll set the whole town agin us."

"Don't worry about that. The whole town will be agin us anyway when the boss moves in on the Double D. Might be some time afore we ride into Hachita again if things turn bad real soon. We might as well enjoy what we can while we can."

"You think the boss will be mad at us?" Clem asked. "Although he tried to make Johnson apologize in public for the way he treated us last time, that don't mean he was pleased at what we did."

"He won't have no choice," Tom asserted. "Caloway needs every gun he can get to work for him right now, and he'll go on needing guns till he's settled into the Double D and run them Randalls out of this county. We're two of the best guns he got. Caloway ain't going to let some women disturb good relations between him and us. Big Pete's no fool."

Clem was doubtful, but as always he went along with what Tom wanted them to do. They headed out for the Johnson place. When they got there, they had a careful look round. Everything looked right. This time they hid their horses so they wouldn't be seen close to the ranch house, tying them beneath a row of old cottonwoods and giving them enough rope so they could graze quietly in the shade unseen. They walked across a hill dotted by small junipers toward the ranch house. Its chimney had blue-gray smoke rising from it.

When Tom shouldered the door in, one of the two girls who was carrying a china bowl of something across the kitchen screamed and dropped it. Whatever was in the bowl —it might have been stewed green peppers—slopped all over the floor, and the bowl cracked in a few pieces. The girl's mother hurried into the kitchen, wiping her hands on her apron, followed closely by her other daughter. They stopped when they saw the two men, and their eyes widened with fear.

"Well, now, ain't this nice?" Tom said. "Here we all are together again."

Clem said nothing. Like the three women, he just stood still and watched Tom, waiting for what he would do next.

When nobody else said anything, Tom went on, "What was we doing when we was interrupted last time? Weren't you going to whistle or sing us a tune, Clem, so I could dance with this purty miss over here? There was something else, too. Yes, I remember. Mrs. Johnson here was kind enough to fetch me a bottle of good bourbon to help us all feel sociable. She fed us, too, now that I remember back. But we ain't asking for food today. You supply the whiskey, Mrs. Johnson, Clem here will provide the music, and this young lady and I will provide the dancing."

Mrs. Johnson found her voice. "Leave your guns on the hall stand."

Tom laughed. "Not this time."

"My husband insists on it. It's a rule of this house."

"When I'm your guest"—Tom tapped himself on the chest—"I make all the rules. Your job is to fetch me the whiskey and whatever else I need."

"You'll drink no liquor in my house with a gun on your hip," she fairly spat at him. "I won't permit it."

Tom walked up to her and looked in her face in a tolerant way. "Get the bottle or I'll go look for it myself while Clem guards you three." He flipped a low table on its side, smashing most of the chinaware that was on it. "I'm kinda clumsy when I go searching for something. You'd save yourself a lot of trouble and aggravation by just bringing it here like I say."

She looked down at the broken stuff knocked from the table, and that decided her. She would take her chances with the whiskey rather than see the contents of her house wrecked before her eyes. She came back in a minute and handed him a bottle two-thirds full of amber liquid.

He twisted the cork out and offered her a swig from the bottle. She shook her head. Then he offered the bottle to each of her daughters and they both declined. Tom took a long toke and handed the bottle to Clem.

"What you going to play for us, Clem?" Tom asked.

"I can whistle 'Clementine.'"

Tom guffawed at the idea of Clem whistling "Clementine." He made one of the daughters dance with him as his pard whistled. Clem paused only for short breaths and quick slugs from the bottle. He gradually went more and more out of tune, and his lips got so puckered it was more like hissing than whistling after a while.

"I can't do it no more," he said finally.

"How about you, Mrs. Johnson?" Tom asked. "Sing us some songs."

"If Mr. Clem behaves like a gentleman and places his gun on the hall stand, I suppose I could relieve him so that he will get to dance too."

Clem willingly unbuckled his gunbelt, laid it on the hall stand by the door, and went up to the second daughter. The mother stared frostily at the Colt still in its holster on Tom's side, but he ignored her. She began to sing lively music hall hits from the time she was a young girl, and the two couples danced around the kitchen more or less in time to her music. Neither of the men saw her open a chest drawer, take something from it, and hold it behind her back.

As she sang, she moved in close to Tom. When he swung by her, she waited till his back was turned to her. Then she brought from behind her back a Smith & Wesson Pocket .32, pulled back the hammer with her left fingers, and discharged the weapon into the small of Tom's back. He dropped like a sack of grain.

Clem ran for the hall stand. She cocked the weapon, fired

at him, missed. Cocked, fired, missed. And again. His hand was on his gun when her fifth bullet from the Smith & Wesson burrowed into his skull below his left eye.

The smoking little pistol in Mrs. Johnson's right hand began to tremble violently. She stood rigidly, still pointing the gun at the hall stand.

"Ma! Ma!" one of her daughters shouted. "Stop singing!"

But she couldn't, not until she came to the end of the song. She had not missed a word or note while gunning down the two intruders with the weapon her husband had hidden for her. When she finished the song, she collapsed weeping on the floor.

Lobo Gonzalez arrived at the Double D ranch house with nearly twenty men. He looked mad as hall. He snarled at Tad Phillips. "You dealing with those Randall coyotes?"

"Lobo, I'm free to deal with anyone I choose," Tad said to him levelly. "Since when did we agree that you have the right—"

"I ain't talking about dealing stock, and you know it," Lobo interrupted. "The Randalls weren't here to buy cattle. They don't buy what they can steal."

"Certainly I'm obliged to you for protecting my stock along with your own," Tad said. "These two Pinkertons know our deal. No, the Randalls weren't here to buy cows, and they weren't paying a social call neither. They told me they'd outbid Pete Caloway on any money he offered, but they weren't prepared to make an honest bid on the land. They agree with Caloway—think I'll be scared off this ranch and the owner will have to sell. Raider asked them if the money they're offering for the Double D came from Greg Peppard's safe. They got mad at that."

So did Lobo Gonzalez. "Half of that money and gold dust they stole belonged to my family and our friends. First our land is stolen by political tricks, and now, after getting the use of it back through an arrangement, it's going to be bought out from under us by someone else using our own gold and cash to dispossess us. We will never stand for it! I will kill them all! What is ours must be returned to us! The deaths of our friends must be avenged!"

Lobo had said another couple of dozen things about blood, vengeance, gold, and land by the time he left the ranch house and gestured to his men to mount their horses.

Watching them leave, Doc said to Tad, "I don't think either Caloway or the Randalls fully understand what they would be up against if they ever succeeded in taking over the Double D. I don't see Lobo doing deals with them."

"If they succeed, he'll have to," Tad said. "They know it, and so does he. That's why he's so damn anxious to stop them. He and his people could never rest easy with any bargain they made with either Caloway or the Randalls. Could be true what you say, though, about Lobo not being willing to deal with the Randalls. But I don't know. Only reason Lobo was willing to deal with me was he got word a U.S. marshal would go after him with a federal posse if he killed me. That was when my uncle was still alive and had friends in Washington. Today nobody outside these parts would give a damn if the Apaches came in and wiped out the lot of us. I reckon the outside world mightn't even miss us for quite a spell."

"If I don't ask for my pay at the end of the month, Chicago will be bound to wonder why," Raider remarked calmly.

"Well, now, that's good," Tad said, "knowing we won't be left lying out here for more than a couple of weeks." He peered out the window. "Now who can this be? I declare I could be out here a month and not see a soul except for the ranch hands, and now all of a sudden it's like living next to

the Sante Fe Trail. A lone rider this time. It's Phil Conners. I
reckon he's here to bring me Caloway's newest threat."

"Maybe not," Raider said. "I told him to come by if he
ever wanted to change jobs."

Tad looked at Raider in surprise. "I'd like to hire him on.
He's a damn good foreman. Just what I need on the Double
D."

"That's what I figured," Raider said with a grin.

Phil Conners brought them the news of what had taken
place in Harry Johnson's ranch house. One of Harry's daughters had ridden into town in search of her father. When Phil
Conners had told Big Pete Caloway about the deaths of his
two men, Caloway had sworn to kill Harry Johnson, even
though Harry hadn't even been there when his wife was
doing the shooting.

"I told Big Pete he could find himself another foreman
then and there," Phil said. "That didn't bother him none. He
had already seen plain enough I wasn't happy with how
things were shaping up. So I rode over to the Johnson place to
warn them about what Caloway had in mind. They was badly
frightened at this, and Harry wanted me to stay and then
wanted to know where I was going. When I told him I was
coming here, he said you, Tad, was a decent man who would
give his family shelter and to tell you they would be right
along after me." He looked around him. "Leastways the
women can clean this place up a bit."

Tad laughed. "They're welcome here. Just so long as they
don't complain about cigar smoke. You wanna work the
Double D as my foreman?"

"I do things my way," Phil warned.

"I probably won't notice your way from any other," Tad
said.

The two men shook hands on it, both knowing that ranching methods were the least of their troubles in the near future.

Raider was tired of this indoors chat and rode out to bring the Johnson family safely in.

Lobo Gonzalez dismounted and handed the reins of his horse to one of his men. He then walked to the top of the hill and squatted down so as not to show a silhouette. Down the far side of the hill was a cluster of old log cabins and pine-board shacks. Lobo remembered that when he was a boy, miners had lived here. They had moved on after the mine had been worked out. The place had been deserted for years before the Randalls moved in. They had built a small corral from scrap lumber for their horses, and a few spare horses worked on the slim pickings on nearby hills. There was no way they could graze a herd of beeves in these bleak hills, which was why they ran them on other men's grass when they owned beasts of their own or stole them when they didn't. Lobo could guess how land-hungry these boys must be and how their mouths must be slavering over the Double D. They were willing to murder for it. They were even willing to die for it.

One of his men crawled alongside him to take a look. Lobo said to him, "No way we can get close enough to pick some of them off without them seeing us first in plenty of time."

"We could charge them from where we are," the man said.

"No, we'd lose too many of our own," Lobo disagreed. "I want to kill our enemies without sacrificing ourselves."

"Every man alive would like to do that."

"Yes," Lobo agreed, "but the Randalls leave us no choice except to try. We passed those freighters a while back on the trail. They have to pass close to these cabins. We'll ride back to them on the far side of this hill, so we're not seen by the Randalls' men."

Four pairs of mules pulled each of three sets of double freight wagons. The freighters sat with their reins and whips on the front edge of the foremost wagons, and a second man rode shotgun alongside each. All six men reached for their weapons when they saw Lobo and his twenty men approach. They hadn't been expecting trouble, since their cargo was mostly foodstuffs—sacks of corn, beans, rice, and flour, along with barrels of oil and pickled goods—bound from Deming to Hachita. The freighters didn't fire, reckoning that Lobo and his men would withdraw when they found that there was nothing light and valuable for them to steal.

Lobo looked back to make sure none of his men had drawn their guns. Then he showed his own hands as a sign of his peaceful intentions. The three freighters and three guards kept them covered with their shotguns and rifles, however, not trusting their show of friendliness.

"We want to ride with you a ways," Lobo shouted to them. "When did you ever hear of me robbing a wagon bound for Hachita?"

"There's always a first time," one freighter said slowly.

"I've got more important things on my mind," Lobo told him. "Be kind enough to pull your teams and rigs close behind each other so my men and I can ride along your left side without being seen from the right."

"You're welcome to use my wagons to sneak up on those sidewinding Randalls," the freighter said, "but you ain't using me as cover to fire behind. These wheels keep rolling no matter what, and you don't start your shooting till you're well clear of us."

Lobo grunted his assent, and he and his men rode in a single line close in to the three teams of mules and the three pairs of wagons. Freight wagons passed by the Randalls' cabins every day on this trail, coming to and from Hachita. Lobo figured that even if the Randalls had men watching the trail closely, they would think nothing of these straining teams of mules, twenty-four in all, pulling the heavy wagons in a swirling cloud of dust that was sometimes so thick it was hard to see more than a few feet. The party moved on like this slowly over the bumpy winding trail.

Lobo finally saw the cabins up ahead through the dust. He gave his men the alert signal and then allowed the wagons to pass almost clear of the cabins before he gave the sign for his men to attack. The horsemen streamed out before and behind the teams and rigs and galloped the short distance to the cabins, levering shells into the chambers of their seventeen-shot Winchester repeaters as they went.

The three Randall men who happened to be about bit the dust in a hail of rifle bullets before they even got a chance to draw their guns. Lobo and his men then shot at random through the windows and open doors of the cabins, downed another two men who came out to face them, and drove the horses out of the rickety corral.

After another fusillade of bullets into the cabins, Lobo and his bunch rode away without any man taking so much as a scrape.

CHAPTER NINE

Tad Phillips picked up his rifle and went outside to look at the rider who was nearing the ranch house. He called to Raider, "It's one of the Randalls' men."

Raider took himself outside when he heard that. He stood next to Phillips, ready to fast-draw if the Randall goon took a notion to put a bullet in Phillips.

"You got the doc here?" the man shouted even before his horse reached them.

"You mean Weatherbee?" Raider asked. "Yeah, he's here."

"We need him bad over at our place. That loco Gonzalez and his bandidos shot us up bad."

Doc Weatherbee came out the door and went into an explanation of his not being a qualified physician and that the Randalls should go into Hachita, where—

"We know all that, Doc," the Randall man said. "We can't go into Hachita 'cause feelings are bad agin us there at the

141

moment. The brothers asked if you'd patch some of our men up so they could be taken to Deming."

Doc always found it hard to refuse when someone seemed to genuinely need his help. "My wagon is in the barn here, and I brought out Judith, my mule, to the ranch also, so I don't have to go into town to get anything. I know where your cabins are. I'll be there in less than a couple of hours."

"I think it's a trap," Tad said.

"If it is a trap, this one will be the first to die," Raider said, pointing to the Randall man. "I'm going along too, and I'll be standing right behind him, so if something goes wrong, he gets a big forty-four in his kidney."

"This ain't a trick," the Randall man said. "Some of us is bleeding real bad, and we're afraid to move them."

More worried by the medical problems facing him than by the danger of a trap, Doc hurried away to hitch Judith to his wagon. Phillips, Conners, the Johnson family, and some of the Double D ranch hands were going to a fandango to be given in the town that evening by allies of Lobo Gonzalez. Raider and Doc said they would head into town from the Randall cabins and meet them there.

Raider and the Randall man rode their horses beside Doc's wagon and made slow but steady progress toward their destination.

"Want me to cut you a thorn stick so you can flay that contrary ole mule and make her pick up her feet?" Raider asked helpfully.

Doc grew angry and said nothing.

Raider told the Randall man conversationally, "That damn mule will be the death of Weatherbee yet. The slower and stupider and meaner the beast gets, the more he puts up with it, instead of laying a stick across the damnfool animal's hide."

Judith turned around to look at Raider with malevolent

eyes and bared her long yellow chisel-shaped teeth at him.

The Randall man was awed. "I do believe that mule understood what you were saying."

"She's smarter than Raider is," Doc commented. "That's what gets him so mad at her."

Six of the Randall men had been killed—three cut down by surprise without a chance to defend themselves, two killed while exchanging fire, and one hit in the head by a shot fired through a cabin window. Three were wounded—one in the chest whom doc did not expect to arrive in Deming alive, one shot in the shoulder who was bleeding bad, and one hit in the leg. Doc managed to staunch the bleeding of the man hit in the shoulder and said he would live if the doctor in Deming could get the bullet out without causing a major infection. The man with the leg wound would be fine in a week. Luke Randall was the only one of the three surviving brothers who had been injured. A bullet had burned an angry red furrow through the skin across his ribs.

"Lucky I stepped aside in the right direction," Luke said to Raider as the Pinkerton dabbed antiseptic ointment on the wound.

Doc was busy with the more seriously hurt men, getting them loaded on a cart to go to Deming, while Raider bandaged Luke Randall's wound.

"Seems like you'll be fighting fit again when I get this here bandage knotted," Raider told him.

"I sure intend to get back at them Gonzalez bastards for what they done to us," Luke said bitterly. "They're just a bunch of thieving bandidos."

"And you're not?" Raider asked with an innocent look.

Luke could hardly get mad at a man still bandaging his wound, so he said, "I know what they say about us being comancheros and all, saying we rustle cattle and are horse thieves. But that's all lies. We're straightforward, honest cattle dealers who work our hands to the bone and get badmouthed by those who envy us. The lazy ones always have the most time to pass judgment on the hardworking ones."

Raider gestured toward a corner in which stood five Sharps rifles. "Were you buffalo hunters at one time?"

Luke grinned. "Them were the days. Over on the Texas plains. Those five guns are the ones us five brothers used. You knew they were buffalo guns, I see. Sharps rifles. Best kind there is for buffalo. You couldn't give Winchesters away for free to buffalo hunters, although they used Henrys, Springfields, Spencers, and Ballards. The Henry and Spencer carbines is fine guns at short range, but a wise man don't come too close to a buffalo herd. The Ballard gives you problems with its ejector. For us, it was choosing between the Remington and the Sharps. Both come in .44−70 and .44−90 calibers. The Remington fires a bottleneck cartridge, while the Sharps is chambered either for it or a straight-sided cartridge. The Remington has a rolling-block breech that is opened by a spur on the top, and the Sharps has a falling breech block activated by the trigger guard. We took the Sharps .44−90 at first. Those guns you see in the corner are all Sharps .40−90−420 caliber, the ones we used later. The .40-caliber bullet weighs 420 grains and is backed by 90 grains of black powder. Each has a walnut stock and a 32-inch barrel and weighs about 12 pounds. I sometimes used a 20-power telescopic sight on mine. Without the telescopic sight, you can hit and kill a bull almost as far as you can see it. At 500 yards, I've had a single bullet pass through three bulls, each standing behind the other, and kill all three of them."

Raider examined one of the rifles. "A friend of mine hunted buffalo up in Wyoming. He preferred the Maynard."

"Fella who rode with us liked the Maynard," Luke said. "I saw him myself—I think it was a .40–70–340 caliber—at maybe 250 yards, I saw him shoot a bull to one side just below the tail and we took the bullet out of the tongue. And that's a buffalo I'm talking about. That Maynard is some gun, though myself I always stuck to the Sharps. For me it was always the boss gun."

Raider had heard Luke speak hardly a word before this. Frank had always been the brothers' spokesman, while the rest of them silently backed him. Raider hadn't expected to find any of the Randalls to be pleasant company. He even sort of liked Luke, so long as he was talking about buffalo hunting.

"Don't you believe none of them pictures you see of a buffalo hunter lying on the ground to aim his rifle," Luke was saying. "Once you fire real close to the ground, the sound of the shot reverberates and could stampede the buffaloes. And you don't know what direction they might decide to run— which is another very fine reason not to be lying on the ground. Buffaloes is such stupid animals, they're liable to run right for whatever it was that spooked them. I always stayed back at least 250 yards so the report of my rifle wouldn't stampede them. I used a stand made of crossed sticks in which to steady my rifle barrel. That way when I brought down one member of the herd, the others wouldn't run away. They'd come over and sniff at the downed animal. Sometimes they'd try to push him upright again with their heads. The more of them you shot, the more came around and did this—so without moving you could pile up their carcasses in one spot ready for the skinners."

"Dirty work," Raider said.

"Skinning was the part of the job my brothers and I tried to avoid," Luke said. "We were getting from two to three dollars a hide, and though this wasn't much, we were willing to split it with the skinners we brought along with us. That was a filthy job. The skinner had to remove the hide from the huge beasts all in one piece, and the hide alone could weigh 150 pounds. He'd be covered with blood and stinking to high heaven, swarming with flies. Then he'd have to scrape off the fat and meat from the inside of the skin before he staked it out on the ground to dry in the sun. When the skins were dry, they were rolled in bundles of ten and put in wagons for the nearest railhead. Some months, when the buffalo wouldn't be around, we'd load carts with their bones from old kills and sell them to be taken back east to make some kind of fertilizer. But that was only in the real hard times when our luck was out. Mostly we did pretty well. Though we was damn glad to take on cattle after that. So when folks ask me how can I be a cattleman since I have no land of my own, I tell them I trained as a buffalo hunter and I don't take no more shit from cattle than I took from buffaloes."

"Except these cattle aren't wild on the range," Raider pointed out. "They belong to someone."

Luke grinned. "Most of them do."

"Well, it ain't my business what you do so long as it don't involve Tad Phillips and the Double D."

"I hear you."

"Mind that you do," Raider said seriously. "Why was that harmless storekeeper Greg Peppard murdered?"

"I wasn't along that night." Luke paused. "Can't say I know anyone who was. But I did hear he was robbed because he was Lobo Gonzalez's banker and that he and his wife got killed by accident."

"By accident?"

"Sure. I heard a man's bandanna was pulled down off his face and he was recognized. Something like that. At the start, nobody was meant to be harmed. Just robbed. Of the bandidos' money."

It was clear enough to Raider now what had happened. Frank Randall was the killer of the old pair.

Doc Weatherbee came up to Raider, looking pleased with himself. "We've done all we can, Raider. You ready to head on into town?"

"Suits me. We better push on before the sun gets low in the sky."

When they were a few paces away, Doc said in an undertone to Raider, "How many able-bodied men do you reckon they have left?"

Raider had already made his count. "Five plus the three brothers."

"Pity Lobo didn't get more of them," Doc muttered. Then he turned around and called to Frank Randall and the others, "I hope next time we meet I won't have to remove bullets from your flesh."

Frank laughed and thanked him.

Raider spoiled the friendly atmosphere by saying, "If they cause trouble on the Double D, the slugs you'll be digging out of them will be mine."

The Hachita community hall was crowded. The musicians were performing on a raised platform at one end—a cornet player, a fiddler, a guitarist, and a drummer. After each dance, men sprinkled the hard-packed adobe earth floor with water to keep the dust down. People sat on wooden benches set against the walls, and small groups gathered around the most attractive girls. *"Den la vuelta,"* the *mayordomo* called at the beginning of each dance, and each couple had to pay a coin as they passed the band the first time. When the dance was over, the man was expected to lead his partner back to the bench where he had found her, wait till she was seated, then bow to her with Spanish courtesy.

Everyone was welcome, Spanish or Anglo. As well as the

townspeople, families had arrived from the outlying ranches, along with cowhands, some miners down from the mountains, and drifters who just happened by. A dozen big men who rode with Lobo Gonzalez circulated through the crowd, saying hello and nodding to their friends, but not dancing, only walking about and watching. When some hell-raiser wandered in from one of the saloons and thought maybe to stir up a row, he would suddenly find himself surrounded by four or five big silent men who would walk him politely out the door. This early in the night, no one was crazy enough yet to try to take them on.

Doc and Raider danced with the Johnson girls under their mother's watchful eye. Cynthia was there, but she was mad at Doc because he had moved out of town to the ranch, and she wouldn't speak or dance with him. Doc was horny as hell, and he could see that nothing was going to work out for him here with the way things were. He decided to join Raider on one of the latter's frequent trips to the saloons, and got stuck talking to an old miner who had scores of long pointless stories and who, with the more whiskey he drank, confused them all together. When Doc asked him if there was much gold in the hills hereabout, the miner said, "Sure, there's tons of gold there, only thing is there's too much damned dirt mixed in with it," and cracked up raucously at his own joke, slapping his knee, hawking up phlegm, and spitting in the sawdust next to Doc's polished boots.

Doc finally had enough and told the miner, "You're drunk, sir, and your stories don't make any sense. We'll have another talk someday when you're sober."

The miner looked Doc in the eye and replied, "Huh, if I was sober, I wouldn't wanna talk to you."

Raider was having a good time. He was off on one of his favorite subjects with some local men and some Southerners

—the War Between the States. Of course he was pleased to introduce Doc to everybody as a damn Yankee, which got Doc a lot of unfriendly looks, though not a single man jack of them there, including Raider and Doc themselves, had been old enough to fight in the conflict. However, Raider was a good Arkansas boy and would never forget—or forgive. To Doc's surprise, he learned that the Civil War had spilled this far to the southwest, down into the New Mexico Territory.

One of the locals was saying, "My pa fought in the Battle of Glorieta, nineteen miles southeast of Santa Fe. One of the most important battles of the whole war, as my pa told it. You ever hear of Glorieta?" he asked, poking his finger in Doc's chest. When Doc politely allowed that he hadn't, the man informed him, "My pa was with the Fourth Texas Volunteers fighting for the Confederacy. On the twenty-eighth day of March in the year 1862, my pa and the Confederates whacked the shit out of Union soldiers at a stagecoach stop known as Pigeon's Ranch. The only thing that stood then between the Confederacy and the goldfields of Colorado and California was Fort Union, twenty-six miles to the north. Damn, with all that gold, the Rebels could have bought all the supplies they needed from Europe, and the North could never have starved them out like they did. If them Rebs had the gold to buy bullets, you wouldn't have them goddamn Yankee carpetbaggers you have today."

"So what happened after the Confederates won at Pigeon's Ranch?" Doc put in, to keep the man from wandering off what he had been talking about.

"The Union soldiers came back next day and beat the tar out of them. My pa was wounded, and that was the end of the war for him, which made my ma and us kids happy. So he never did get to Fort Union, and the Confederacy never did get the Colorado and California gold."

"A story with a happy ending," Doc remarked and moved away while Raider prevented the man from coming after him.

This time Doc saw a pretty woman at the fandango who had not been there before. She was small, curvy, with lots of black curly hair, an excellent dancer. She told him her name was Alicia, that her husband had been killed a year before by the Apaches, that she had left her two children with her sister who was married to one of Lobo Gonzalez's men, that she was tired of mourning, that she was in town for a good time. Doc set about giving her one. They stopped dancing only to refresh themselves at one of the saloons. They were at a table in the Cottonwood Inn when the Randalls hit the community hall.

The three Randalls figured that no one would be able to prove it was them, since they and their five men wore bandannas covering their faces and it was by now full dark with the only illumination coming from oil lamps hung on strings between trees in the plaza. At first it seemed crazy for eight mounted men to attack a community hall with more than 150 people in it, more than half of them armed men, but they had method in their madness. The five men galloped around the plaza, coming close to the hall, firing wildly from their rifles and pistols. The crowd in the community hall and outside it thought that the men were firing at random into them, which was what they were supposed to think, and they panicked and rushed for the exits, which was what they were supposed to do.

Meanwhile, in a dark place toward the center of the plaza the three Randall brothers waited side by side with their Sharps buffalo rifles, scanning the crowd milling beneath the oil lamps strung between the trees.

A man's face exploded an arm's length from Lobo Gonzalez as he emerged from the hall, and a second man was hit in the throat as Lobo ducked into the crowd and zigzagged away. Two women were grazed by a single bullet next to Big Pete Caloway, and a third bullet tore the Stetson from his head as he ran through the crowd for cover.

Raider spotted right off that the five men, staying out of easy gunsight by moving in and out of the shadows and riding fast, were only firing above the heads of the crowds to frighten them. The five were cowhands and knew how to drive cattle. This time they were whipping a confused herd of humans back and forth in the square. Then Raider saw the muzzle flames of rifles in the center of the plaza. He didn't know who these men were or who they were shooting at or why, but he could see that they weren't shooting harmlessly above the heads of the people to panic them. They were searching for particular targets and sniping for them only. As the men continued to select their shots, and fear grew in the crowd as they saw actual victims of bullets among them, Raider raced through the darkness toward the center of the plaza. The rifle bullets the three men were firing whistled over his head toward the crowd behind him.

Raider could see by now the shadowy outlines of three mounted men. Intent on searching in the crowd beneath the oil lamps for targets, they had not seen Raider coming close to them through the darkness. The three men had rifles; he had only his Remington .44 revolver. There was no cover in the center of the plaza, except the blackness of the night. It would be no contest—three rifles versus a revolver—if they could see him. Yet he had to get within thirty or so paces of them to make his revolver aim effective under these conditions.

"There's Tad Phillips!" one of the horsemen snarled. "Back toward the corner of the wall. Nail the two-faced skunk!"

Raider recognized the voice. Frank Randall's. He was the

one to the right, and Raider saw his dark form hunch down on his rifle to take a shot at Phillips. There was no time now for the Pinkerton to worry about getting close enough for accuracy. He fast-drew and rapid-fired three shots at the smaller form atop the larger dark form of the horse. Hit or miss, Raider reckoned at least he'd throw off Frank Randall's aim and save Tad's life.

Three shots fired, Raider ran a dozen steps to the left and two of the rifles spat bullets in the place he had been. Raider eased open the revolving chambers of the .44 and silently ejected the cartridges spent and loaded. He had no choice but to crouch silently and do this because he had only two bullets left in his gun. Before the dance, he had pulled a cartridge from the chamber that would rest directly beneath the firing pin, so that if the hammer was jolted or the gun knocked to the floor, the pin would strike on an empty chamber. An empty chamber and three shots fired left two cartridges against the riflemen just a short distance away. He knew that he no longer faced three men because he heard them talk as he inserted fresh shells in the chambers.

"Frank! Frank!"

"You all right?"

"Speak to me, Frank."

"Hold my horse while I take a look. Watch for that snake. He's out there somewhere, right under our noses." There was silence for a spell. "He's dead, Luke. Frank's dead. He ain't breathing."

"Git up on your hoss, man," Luke said.

Moments later they clattered away across the plaza toward the dark end of the town. Raider's gun was loaded by now, but he wasted no shots by firing wildly after them, a dangerous thing to do anyway in the town. The riderless horse ran a nervous circle around him in the dark as he searched for Frank, wary of a trap. The other five riders

abandoned their crowd-scaring tactics once they noticed the
other two ride off. They headed in the opposite direction.
Raider listened intently. Above the excited voices of the
crowd, a good distance away, he could hear nothing near him
except the anxious padding of the horse's hooves. He moved
forward slowly into the pitch darkness, feeling on the ground
before him with his feet, his Remington .44 cocked and
leveled in his right hand.

A foot touched something. He gently kicked it. It rolled a
little under the pressure of his boot, like a body would. He
bent down and groped with his left hand. It touched a nose
and forehead and eyes, hot and wet. He raised his hand and
smelled his palm. It smelled of blood.

Six or seven people had been killed and twice that number
injured before the horsemen rode away. Doc Weatherbee
assisted the town doctor in helping the wounded, and Alicia
helped as a nurse. When they had done all they could, they
slumped away exhausted, Doc having assured himself that
Raider, Tad Phillips, and everyone staying at the Double D
were all right. Alicia had been lent a small house for the night
by a cousin. It faced onto the plaza and was only a short walk
away.

When they went inside, Alicia lighted an oil lamp. The
place was very nicely decorated. "This was supposed to be
my love nest on my big night out," she said sardonically.
"I'm tired now, all I'm capable of is flopping into that bed
and sleeping."

A gentleman as always, Doc offered to join her.

She went behind a screen to change and emerged in a lacy
white nightgown. She lay back on the bed, stretched her arms
and legs luxuriously, and yawned. Doc dimmed the lamp,
leaving it burning on a low wick. He stripped off his clothes,
being careful to get the crease in his pants legs even, and

joined her on the bed, not forgetting to remove his derby.

She had nice little tits, round and soft, with erect hard nipples. He pulled down her nightgown and kissed each nipple as tenderly as he could, then flicked his tongue over and around them. His right hand eased the nightgown down over her hips and then glided over her flat belly, which felt firm and silky. He took each of her breasts in his mouth and sucked on her nipples hard. She offered herself to him, sighing with pleasure.

Alicia seemed to forget her exhaustion as Doc's expert fingers caressed the most sensitive parts of her body. But Doc himself was not looking for any sex marathon tonight. He wanted a good pleasant fuck and a night's heavy sleep. He would see about the athletics and gymnastics in the morning.

He entered her with his stiff rod, and she grabbed him by the hips and pulled him into her. Her snatch was tight though moist, and he had to force his way all the way in. When he had gone all the way, he paused with his dick deep inside her—and then, very slowly and gently, he began moving.

She moved with him rhythmically, and in time the pace of their fucking grew more fervent till they were frantically humping each other. She had a violent orgasm, twisting about on his cock and shouting something in Spanish. Moments later Doc himself shot his hot jism deep inside her.

Panting and sated, they slipped together into a deep sleep.

CHAPTER TEN

Doc and Alicia were too busy with their own involvements and finally too deep in sleep to notice the sounds of what was happening on the other side of the plaza from Alicia's cousin's house. After Luke and Bart Randall abandoned the dead body of their brother Frank in the center of the plaza, they headed for a narrow alley which led onto the main trail back to their cabins. This was where they ran into a surprise set by two twelve-year-old boys to torment some visitors to the fandango, preferably with a skinful of rotgut. They had stretched an old lariat across the alley, pulled taut and tied at each end to the iron bars outside windows in adobe houses. They set the rope about chest-high to a riding man, high enough to clear the top of a big stallion's head. As Luke and Bart galloped out of the plaza into the alley, first Luke and then Bart were lifted from the saddle, suspended in air for a moment as their horses ran from beneath them, and then deposited hard in a sitting position on the packed earth of the alley.

The two boys, who had concealed themselves on a nearby adobe roof to view the fun, were silent for a moment in the darkness. They had seen what had happened in the plaza, and now they suddenly saw themselves transformed from pranksters into possible heroes for apprehending these gunmen. They raised a holler from the rooftop, the townsmen came running, and the two limping brothers who had lost their horses were found on the edge of town. The marshal tried to assert his authority and take them to the town jail, but Big Pete Caloway roused the crowd into a fury at the two men, pointing out what they had done this night, summing up a few of the things they and their brothers were believed to have done at previous times, and pointing out that no one could consider his life safe until all five of the Randall brothers had been removed from the face of God's earth. Big Pete Caloway held up the old lariat that the two boys had used to unhorse the Randalls and suggested that it be put to one further use.

Marshal Miguel Santiago stepped in at this point and, with the help of two deputies, forcibly took Luke and Bart Randall away from Caloway and his supporters. The marshal stowed the two prisoners in a cell at the back of his office and left them in the charge of one of the deputies while he and the other deputy searched for Lobo Gonzalez to ask him for some men as instant temporary deputies to quiet the lynch mob.

While the marshal was gone, the deputy in charge was relieved when things quieted down of a sudden. But not for long. He heard a woman screaming for help outside in the plaza. When he flung open the door to go to her aid, he found himself looking into the muzzles of five pistols. The men, all locals whom he knew, backed him into the office. One tried to open the door that led to the cells.

"It's locked. Give us the key."

"The marshal's got it," the deputy lied. "He didn't leave it with me. It's no good—there's no way you can get at the prisoners."

More than twenty men were crowded into the office by now, and more were standing in the plaza outside, demanding to know what was going on. Caloway was outside with them, loudly demanding that harsh justice be dealt out. One man inside the office came up to the locked door with a can of kerosene. He pulled the bung out.

"We'll douse this place and put a match to it," he said. "That way at least we'll hear the fuckers screaming when the flames get to them."

"No! No!" the deputy shouted. "There are three drunks in there and another man held for questioning. You can't kill them!"

"Who's gonna miss 'em?" the man with the can asked, which brought a rumble of go-aheads from the men there.

"I'll give you the key!" the deputy offered and went to its hiding place beneath the marshal's desk.

The man with the can winked behind the deputy's back to the others and turned the can upside down to show them it was empty.

The deputy unlocked the door. "I don't have the key to their cell, and I'm telling you the truth there."

Bart and Luke Randall sat on a wooden bench at the back of the cell, looking out through the bars at the townsmen crowded into the narrow corridor.

"All right, men," a voice shouted. "We have the rats cornered, and we should all be in this together."

Luke and Bart looked at the revolver barrels poking in the bars at them. Their cold blue eyes were calm, as if this was something they had been expecting to happen for a long time. They neither looked at nor spoke to each other before the pistols barked and their bodies jerked from the multiple impacts and slumped off the bench onto the stone cell floor.

Big Pete Caloway slipped away down the plaza from the mob outside to the marshal's office a few minutes after the shooting of the two Randalls. He went into the Western Union telegraph office and spent some time composing a telegram.

> Col. Herbert Turpin
> U.S. Fifth Cavalry
> Fort Grady
> New Mexico Territory

> Situation in Hachita has deteriorated. Essential that cavalry come immediately to quell insurrection by forces of Lobo Gonzalez. Attack mounted tonight on community hall, many dead and wounded. Prisoners later shot in town jail with complicity of marshal appointed by Gonzalez. Further deaths will result unless immediate relief is sent.

> Caloway

He had to wait some time for the telegraph clerk to send out a long message for a man with a Spanish accent. This telegram was the strongest of a series that Caloway had sent the colonel about the troubles in Hachita. He hoped the colonel wouldn't remember that most of his previous complaints had been directed at the Randalls. The colonel had almost sent troops once before, except an attack by Apaches made them needed more desperately somewhere else. With luck, the colonel would send troops this time. The Randalls were gone, so Caloway would meet them and direct them against Gonzalez and his men. With Gonzalez gone, or a least with his strength broken, Caloway would rule the roost after the troopers left. He knew that Tad Phillips was conniving with Lobo, and that before he could hope to join the Lazy K and the Double D into his own vast cattle empire he would have to eliminate the threat that Lobo presented. With the Randalls gone and Lobo gone or beaten down, it would be a breeze.

When the telegraph clerk finished the previous man's message, he got around to sending out Caloway's. Big Pete stuck around to make sure it went out without a hitch and that the entire transmission was acknowledged as received by the other end. Only then did he consider it a night's work well done.

Raider and some others had taken over from the town doctor and Doc Weatherbee in watching over the wounded members of the crowd outside the fandango. There was no shortage of extra volunteers, so when Raider heard about the mob killing the last two Randalls, he left the community hall, where the wounded were being cared for, and headed along the plaza toward the marshal's office. One hell of a commotion was going on there. After discovering it was true that Luke and Bart, as well as Frank, Randall were dead, he felt in need of getting away from the excited mob and the whole noisy town. He picked his way though some back streets to the edge of town, realizing he couldn't go far because of the pitch blackness of the night. He saw a lamp higher on the hillside and decided he would climb up that far at least.

It was tough going in the dark, but that gave Raider something to think about besides the goings-on in the town. He was surprised when he came to the cemetery wall and saw that the lamp was hanging on a picket fence surrounding a grave. He could see no one in its light, but he clearly heard the scrape of a shovel in soil. He figured that so many had been killed in the town tonight, the gravediggers were getting an early start on all the holes they would have to dig. He climbed over the wall and wended his way through the graves to talk with them.

Only one man was working there. He was more than knee-deep in a hole, methodically shoveling the earth in a pile to one side. Raider hadn't seen him at first because he was outside the bright yellow circle of lamplight.

"Getting ready for tomorrow?" Raider called from some distance away so as not to startle the man. He reckoned that not even a gravedigger would care to have a figure appear suddenly from the darkness close to him. Maybe especially not a gravedigger.

The man looked at him dourly and said, "The bitch ain't here."

"What ya say?" Raider came closer, puzzled.

"They claim I murdered her. Say I stabbed her with my knife. I thought I'd killed the bitch too. But no way. She laid a curse on me, mister. The healers told me the curse would last as long as she's alive. When I saw her dead, I thought the curse was finally gone. Right?"

"Sure, sure." Raider remembered: El Mellado, the toothless one who had murdered his wife and escaped from jail.

His eyes lit up in the lamplight like those of a chess player about to deliver a great move. "But you see, I still have the curse, so I know she is still alive. Can you understand the venom of her joke? She is still alive, while I get blamed for her death and still have to bear her curse. I know she is laughing at me. I can hear her terrible laugh."

Raider began, "Now, look here, old buddy—"

"You think I'm loco too? Everyone thinks I am crazy. Lobo Gonzalez won't let me carry a gun." He slapped his holsterless right hip. "So what can I do? What? I have to show them. But they don't want me to. It is too much trouble for them to listen. Who cares what crazy old El Mellado says? Since they won't listen with their ears, I must give them something for their eyes to see. Then they cannot deny the truth of what I say!"

Raider didn't say anything. He knew that El Mellado was wanted for murder, but this didn't count for much, since Lobo Gonzalez had been protecting him and Marshal Santiago was Lobo's man. But he couldn't just go away and leave this insane man to dig his dead wife's body out of the ground. The marshal and his deputies had more than enough troubles in the town tonight—they couldn't leave to come out here to deal with a loony.

"When I break that coffin open," El Mellado was shouting, chopping with the shovel blade, "and when everyone sees the coffin is empty, then they will know that the witch is still hidden somewhere among them, watching them with sly eyes, working her evil ways."

"Look, I ain't saying you're wrong and I ain't saying you're right," Raider tried. "All I'm saying is this is one helluva time of night to try this. You'll need witnesses or no one will believe you, and you're not going to get witnesses to come here in the middle of the night. Why don't you do this tomorrow afternoon? I want you to quit and go home now."

"Never!" El Mellado's wide eyes blazed defiance.

Raider sighed, then said, "G'wan, git!"

El Mellado waved the shovel threateningly at him.

The Pinkerton advanced on him. When he saw that Raider was going to take him on, shovel or no shovel, he dropped it and lay on his back in the grave. "You'll never get me outta here. You can even bury me if you want."

Raider picked up the shovel and drove it into the pile of earth at the side of the hole. He heaved a shovelful into the grave. Then another. And another. El Mellado stood up in the grave, climbed out, and ran away into the darkness among the crosses and picket fences. Raider ignored him and continued to fill in the grave by lamplight.

"Crazy is crazy," he muttered to anyone who might be listening in the quiet graveyard, "but a shovelful of earth in the face brings any man to his senses."

The sun was high before Big Pete Caloway got a reply to his emergency telegram to the U.S. Cavalry colonel. Caloway had been to the Western Union office a couple of times before it arrived. When it did finally come and the clerk had finished setting it down in his neat copperplate handwriting, he ran into the plaza outside the Western Union office and waved the sheet of yellow paper to attract Caloway's attention. Caloway was examining a cut on the foreleg of one of his men's horses, and he hurried expectantly to the telegraph office, knowing the clerk could not leave his post to bring the message to him. He gave the clerk a silver dollar for his trouble and read the telegram.

Your latest message received re conditions in Hachita. Your concern over conditions has been shared here to such an extent that a Capt. P. Iglesias was despatched in civilian clothes to your location for the purposes of reconnaissance and assessment. His report preceded yours by minutes. He mentions your name in connection with the jailhouse incident. Further, he attributes troubles to the Randall faction, which is no longer extant. In view of his report, no immediate U.S. action against Gonzalez et al. seems necessary. Whether the Army acts against other segments of interest in this series of disputes will be decided by future events.

H. Turpin, Col., U.S. Fifth Cavalry

"That Captain Iglesias musta been the shithead who was

sending out that long telegram before me," Caloway said to one of his men. "Lobo must have bribed the skunk. Them greasers all stick together."

"Captain who?" the man asked, not having read the telegram.

"Never mind."

The threat implied in the last sentence of the colonel's telegram was not lost on Caloway. He had been mistaken to think a career officer would back him as a matter of course, since he was a landowner, against such scum as the Randalls and Lobo Gonzalez. Caloway knew he had no time to waste in tangling with the Army bureaucracy or with Washington politicians. In a place as isolated as Hachita, by the time some distant authority handed down its considered decision, the matter usually had been long decided locally. Possession being nine-tenths of the law, as the proverb went, Caloway was convinced that once he took over the Double D, it almost certainly could not be taken from him. Certainly there would be reparations to be paid, but these would be well below the value of the land, and as such would not be difficult to get a bank to finance. There was no way a couple of hired Pinkertons and an armchair rancher like Tad Phillips could stop him from grabbing the land, Big Pete was sure of that. The Randalls were gone. All that stood between him and the Double D now was Lobo Gonzalez—plus Lobo's men and his handpicked marshal in town, Miguel Santiago.

With the colonel making a veiled threat toward him in the telegram, Caloway decided that the marshal, as the figurehead of law and order in Hachita, could prove to be a dangerous individual, with the very real power of summoning outside aid, Apaches permitting. Miguel Santiago might be the best person he could remove right away, and put in his own man as the new marshal, as the Randalls had done before Gonzalez followed their example. That way, he would

at least control the town—and if he couldn't cut off supplies
completely to Lobo and his bunch in the hills, he could have
it made plain to them there was no welcome for them in
Hachita.

He was thinking that this made a lot of sense when one of
his men rode up to him in a hurry.

"We got four fellas down here want to talk with you, boss.
They say Frank Randall owes them a week's pay, and if you
wanna pay 'em what they is owed, then they work for you.
We sure could use a few extra guns, and these is mighty
serious fellas."

"Where are they?" Caloway asked.

"On a side street a little ways down. They don't want to
ride into the plaza till they're sure folks won't go shooting
them."

Caloway mounted his horse and rode with his man to
where the four men were waiting in their saddles. Big Pete
nodded to them and said, "The money ain't no problem. I'll
give you what the Randalls owed you and pay you from now
on twenty dollars a week more. There was five of you riding
around the plaza, shooting over the crowd. Where's the fifth
man?"

"He took off. We didn't shoot no one. It was the Randalls
done that. But he figured they'd be just as likely to string us
up or shoot us in the town cells, like they done to Luke and
Bart."

"That was a dirty low-down trick," Big Pete said insin-
cerely. "I dunno if the locals think you lot killed people or
not. I got a right to be mad too. You knew I was one of the
ones the Randalls wanted to kill. What made you think I'd
want to hire you now?"

"Ain't nothing personal in this, mister. We work for the
one who pays us."

"Good," Caloway said. "That'll be enough for me. You

four will stay with us out at the Lazy K. I'll pay you your last week's wages soon as we get there. But before we ride out of town, I need your help to take care of a simple matter— meaning the marshal. He works for Gonzalez, so he's gotta go."

Caloway, his man, and the four new recruits rode back into the plaza and along to where three more of his men waited with their horses. Eight men and himself were what he had in town. It was almost midday—there was a good chance they'd take the marshal by surprise. By day's end he'd have his own man in the job. He gave his fellow riders instructions as they rode along the edge of the plaza toward the marshal's office. It would be brutal, simple, and quick— the best way to get a thing done, in Caloway's way of thinking.

They rode loosely strung out, unhurried, with orders not to go for their guns till outside the marshal's office. A few buildings before the office, Caloway saw a man squatting with a rifle on the flat roof of an adobe house. One of Lobo's bandidos. There was another on the next building. Another on the next. Two on the flat roof of the marshal's office. More on the buildings on the far side.

Big Pete didn't have to give his men any signals to call off the attack. They had eyes in their heads as well as he. He just kept riding past, and his men followed him, peaceful as anyone could wish, all the way out of town.

They heard the warning shots, and men tumbled from the bunkhouse and the ranch house kitchen. Most of them were wearing revolvers, some had their long guns close by, others were able to get to them. When Big Pete Caloway saw the band of horsemen approaching and thus realized that the warning was a real emergency, he hurried his wife and children, the cook, and the housekeeper down into a root cellar a short distance from the house, where they would be safe from stray bullets.

The group of riders galloping toward the Lazy K spread out, making themselves harder to hit. They rode low over their horses' necks, firing their rifles as they came and spattering bullets off the ranch house, bunkhouse, and barn, which were all close together, almost joining one another.

Caloway recognized one man. Then another. The Gonzalez bunch! Then he saw what their purpose was. At least three of the riders carried long tree branches with a bunch of flaming rags, no doubt soaked in kerosene, at one end. They weren't going to continue their frontal attack on the ranch house, as they wanted Big Pete and his men to believe. Pete knew they would veer behind the bunkhouse to the barn, set fire to it, and gallop away. He gestured urgently to four or five men to follow him, and they ran between the barn and the ranch house, but already the Gonzalez horsemen had passed behind the bunkhouse. There was no way now they could intercept them before they got to the barn. The most they could do was avenge themselves on the riders when they passed it.

Lobo and his riders were not expecting them. They thought they had made a complete surprise attack, fired the barn, and made a clean getaway.

"Fire for their horses!" Caloway yelled to his men, knowing that once the bigger, easier targets were downed on the open grassland, the men brought down with them could be picked off with ease.

A lucky shot brought down one of the lead horses in a tight-knit bunch that had formed in the getaway. The wounded horse stumbled on all four legs and skidded on its side on the grass, raising its head and kicking wildly. This horse unseated its rider and brought three other horses down, one of which brought another two horses down. These five horses, all uninjured by their falls and not hit by bullets, were on their legs again in seconds and galloped on—but with empty saddles.

Another two horses were hit by rifle bullets, and both sank back on their haunches, thrashing in pain and fear. The two riders leaped clear of their mounts' crushing body weight and flailing hooves. They were hardened men, expert with horse and gun, and they held on to their weapons as they were flung onto the ground.

All told, eight of the Gonzalez bunch were caught on the open grassland, along with three dying horses. Two of the men were lying on the ground, moving but unable to stand. The other six ran to take cover behind the downed horses, which were all trying to struggle to get upright. The less successful the horses were in standing, the more panicked they became, and they kicked and twisted so savagely that the men couldn't get near enough to them to gain cover from the Lazy K rifles. Caloway and his men blasted away at them.

"Come on!" Big Pete yelled. "Kill all these bastards before they can be rescued!"

The rest of the Gonzalez bunch had wheeled their horses about and were coming back fast, their rifle bullets peppering the barn and ranch house walls behind Big Pete and his men. But Caloway had the eight men caught. He and the others brought four down in just a few seconds. Two managed to find some cover behind a struggling horse, and it took a little longer to finish them off. Which left only the two wounded men. One was firing at them from where he lay with his revolver. He took a bullet in the midriff, another in the thigh, and two high in the chest, all from different guns, with all the slugs hitting him almost simultaneously, puncturing his flesh and tearing through his vital tissues.

The second wounded man sat up and looked at them,

knowing his fate yet wanting to show them he could die unafraid. The Gonzalez bunch was bearing down on them, and Big Pete wondered for an instant what was keeping his men from plugging this last of the eight and getting back behind cover. Then he saw who the wounded man was. It was Lobo Gonzalez himself! They had him! And Big Pete's men were leaving him for their boss to kill himself.

Pete's heart warmed toward his men for their generosity as he picked up the bead of his front sight in the notch of his rear sight. The bead was sitting on Lobo's mouth. Pete could hear the hooves of the Gonzalez bunch come back for their leader. He squeezed the trigger.

Lobo's face blew apart. Caloway was so exultant, he didn't even feel the heat of his barn burning behind his back.

CHAPTER ELEVEN

Big Pete Caloway was feeling pressure. The barn fire had spread to the ranch house and bunkhouse, and all the Lazy K had left were three rectangles of blackened smoldering timber. Even most of the rails of the corrals and pens had burned to ash. No lives had been lost because of the fire. His wife, kids, and two women servants had been badly frightened but were unharmed. He had sent them to stay up in Deming till all this was over. One of his men had been shot dead by the Gonzalez raiders, another had died of a chest wound a few hours later, and two other men had taken flesh wounds which disabled neither of them. Lobo was dead. Apart from the seven who died with him, another two had been killed in the attempted rescue of their downed leader.

Before sundown that evening, Big Pete led his men in an attack on the Gonzalez compound in the foothills. In spite of his rage, Caloway saw that this attack was foolhardy. The Gonzalez crowd were too well entrenched and over the years had come to know all the ins and outs of defending their position. Caloway called off his men before he lost any and before they had inflicted any damage. On the way back to the Lazy K, they paid the marshal another visit. He still had sharpshooters posted on the roofs of the nearby adobes, and there was no way they could go against those from the open plaza. They left town peacefully and headed back to the smoking embers of what had once been the Lazy K.

Caloway refused to allow his men to stay in town or to move to the cabins the Randalls had occupied. In either place they would be too far removed from where Caloway wanted them to be. But it wasn't summer yet, and sleeping out under the stars was not all that easy to do with teeth chattering from the cold. And so the pressure built on Big Pete. It forced him to decide quickly that any further hassles with the Gonzalez bunch or with Marshal Santiago in town was a waste of valuable effort. The leaderless Gonzalez bandidos would find someone to take over, but whoever it was, he would need time to establish his authority and earn the respect of the others. By that time Big Pete would be firmly set up on the Double D. The marshal in Hachita had no jurisdiction over what went on out on the ranches beyond the town limits. He couldn't be much more than an annoyance to them when they had to go to town. If it came to that, Big Pete knew he could avoid Hachita altogether for a spell and bring in supplies directly from Deming. This would be troublesome and expensive but worthwhile if it kept him and Lobo's sympathizers far apart for a while.

That's what he would do—forget about the Gonzalez bunch. Lobo was dead. For a time at least, they could give him no trouble, until they got themselves organized. From that viewpoint, the Gonzalez raid on the Lazy K had turned into a victory for Big Pete Caloway. He had lost the buildings on the Lazy K, but he had intended to move out of them anyway into the much larger quarters at the Double D when he merged both spreads. The only disadvantage he had picked up, Caloway decided, was that he now had his men sleeping in the open and eating from a chuckwagon. However, they were cowhands and used to this. Still, it would be nice to see a ceiling over his head pretty soon, Pete decided.

He got ten of his men to ride with him to the Double D. To show that his intentions were honorable, he left his men at the Double D corral and walked from there to the ranch house.

"Don't let him in," Doc Weatherbee told Tad Phillips. "I don't want him to see how we have things set up in here or who's in here and who's in the bunkhouse or the barns. Talk to him outside the door."

Raider went outside the ranch house with Tad to meet with Caloway.

"Ain't you going to invite me in out of the sun?" Big Pete asked Tad.

"Sorry, Pete, you and me ain't good neighbors anymore."

"Pity to hear that, Phillips, but if that's how you want it, that's how it will be. I came over here on a friendly mission, thinking I could still give you a chance to save your bacon by moving on outta here. These two detective agency dudes ain't going to be no match for the men I got. And that little turncoat traitor Phil never was no good to handle a gun anyhow. He's no loss to me, and by the same token he ain't no great gain to you. I know you got Harry Johnson in there. You think he's going to be of help to you? Shit! Only reason he's in there is because he's afeared of me anyhow. And you, Tad Phillips, it's high time you was thinking about yourself. This ain't even your land. You going to die to protect someone else's property? I could understand a man being willing to sacrifice his life for what he owns, especially his land. But they're gonna laugh at you as a damnfool for spilling your blood on this rich widow woman's ranch. She don't even care about this place. She owns several other places where she don't have no troubles like she has down here. Take my word for it, she'll be happy to see the last of this place."

Tad said nothing and looked expectantly at Raider for him to make some response. Raider just grinned, like they were all the best of friends just passing the time with some silly talk. Caloway was ignoring the existence of the big Pinkerton, addressing all his remarks to Tad. But Raider was too looming a presence for Caloway's tactic to be convincing. A man might as well try to pretend a nearby grizzly didn't exist.

Tad pulled himself together. "In spite of all your talk being phrased to sound like good advice from one man to another, it seems to me that you're just plain making threats against me, Caloway. All I can say is, do your worst. But I warn you, it's going to be an eye for an eye, an arm for an arm. If I'm not going to live out this fight, you can bet your ass you won't either."

Caloway looked at the smaller man with contempt. "You're just a little boy talking big when you got your friend standing next to you. You know this ain't how you really feel, Tad. You're scared inside. Real bad."

"Sure I am," Tad said with fire in his eyes, "and that's why I'll survive. You're such a cock o' the rock, you're going to walk into a bullet real soon when you're not looking."

Big Pete laughed at the notion of Tad Phillips threatening him. "All right, Phillips, it's war from now on. You better tell your men they ain't safe to ride your herds or go into town for a drink or a woman. See how long they'll stay with you when they hear we're gunning for Double D ranch hands. You gonna have an empty bunkhouse in a matter of hours. What happens then? You gonna get that city slicker Weatherbee to punch cattle for you? Rustlers will wipe your spread clean of stock within a week, soon as word gets out. You got problems, Tad. Along with the fact of your not wanting to die for

me rich bitch's property who won't say thanks to you one
ay or another. I'm telling you, boy, let's stay friends. You
de outta these parts along with these two Pinkertons. Take
hil Conners with you. Harry Johnson and me will make
iends. I'll pay the widow woman more than she deserves.
Vhy you wanna end up bleeding in the dirt for a shit deal like
iis? Tell me now. I'm listening."

"Only 'cause you ain't gonna scare me off, Caloway,"
ad said. "You figure you can. It's worth it to me to show you
iat you can't."

"You been talking to the wrong people, Tad. They been
iisleading you real bad."

"Could be," Tad allowed. "We'll find all that out pres-
ntly."

Big Pete shook his head, like he felt sorry he couldn't
eep Tad from destroying himself by making this terrible
iistake. He walked away slowly and sadly. Suddenly he
irned, causing Raider's right hand to float like a butterfly
bove the handle of his big Remington .44. But Caloway was
ot going for his gun. He was pointing his forefinger at Tad,
is face contorted with rage.

"Your ass is grass," he spat.

"I was a *mayordomo* of an *acequia* district," the old man
old Raider.

The two Pinkertons had sneaked into town for a little
iversion, figuring the Double D was safe enough after
undown. Caloway and his men had plenty to do camping out
> keep their minds busy till sunup. Doc was playing faro for
>w stakes at a gaming table in the Cottonwood Inn. Raider
/as at the bar, drinking and talking.

"I know a *mayordomo* is kinda like a manager or fore-
aan," Raider said to the old Spanish man. "What's an *ace-
uia* district?"

"This was up by Velarde, on the Rio Grande north of Sante Fe. Area had five *acequia* districts. I was *mayordomo* of one of them. I quit two years ago. Got too old for the work. Legs gave out mostly, so my nephew took over the job. He's a good lad. Hardworking. Don't drink. Hell, I didn't drink for years neither, till things got to me. Anyways I'm back here now. I was born in Hachita; going to die here too."

"What's an *acequia* district?" Raider asked patiently.

The old man looked at him suspiciously. "You're sure given to asking questions, stranger. You doubt the truth of what I been saying to you?"

Raider laughed at the cantankerous man and poured him whiskey from his bottle. This seemed to lighten the atmosphere.

"An *acequia* district," the old man said thoughtfully. "You know, you're the first man I've ever met who didn't know what an *acequia* district was."

"They don't have 'em in Arkansas."

"Just about this time of year, maybe a bit earlier, when the sun starts melting the snow off the Sangre de Cristo Mountains, I'd take twenty-five, maybe thirty men with shovels along the ditches—that's what an *acequia* is, an irrigation ditch—and we'd get rid of all the debris collected over the winter, cut back willow branches, lift out rocks, and break up beaver dams so the water would have a clear passage. Now the users of the water are the ones who pay into an association in each *acequia* district, and the *mayordomo* is the one who decides where the water is most needed and who gets how much of it."

The old man rattled on, telling Raider more than the Pinkerton ever wanted to know about irrigation systems and about his own importance as a *mayordomo*. He was explaining how he used a measuring rod called a *vara* when Raider noticed two men watching him and talking together. He was sure he had seen one of them before, riding with Big Pete Caloway. Then the two men separated. One came to the bar a few places down from him on one side and the other also came to the bar to order a drink but on Raider's other side and not so close to him. If he had to face one, he had to turn his back on the other. Doc was concentrating on his faro game and saw nothing. The old man was still channeling irrigation water in his mind, and although he wore a gun, he was probably long past being able to use one effectively. Raider sipped his drink, holding the glass in his left hand now, keeping his gun hand free, and waited.

He didn't have long to wait. The one closest to him shouted at him across the two men who were between them. Raider didn't hear what he said. It sounded none too friendly. The two men between them looked from Raider to Caloway's man and back a few times before they picked up their bottles and glasses and ambled down to a more peaceable section of the bar. The man said something again to Raider which Raider again did not catch because of the background noise.

"You talking to me?" Raider asked, turning around so that his back was to the bar. He turned his head to the right to talk with this man and quickly turned his head back to glance out of his left eye at the other man. That hombre was watching and no doubt ready to help the talking one by backshooting Raider if he could. The old man was on his left—being washed down a ditch by the big spring floods of eleven years ago.

"You the Pinkerton fella staying out on the Double D?" the man asked.

"One of them."

"Big Pete asked me to give you something."

Raider smiled in his relaxed way, glanced fast at the man down the bar to the left of him, then turned his head to the right again, keeping his back to the bar. "I got a shrewd idea of what it could be that Big Pete was asking you to give me. It comes in a caliber of close to half an inch."

"You got the right idea, mister. I'm ready when you are."

"Anytime," Raider said, friendly and unconcerned.

Both men moved away a little down from the counter. There was a rattle of glasses as customers took their bottles and glasses to safety along with themselves.

Knowing he had two men to handle, one on either side of him, Raider was not going to let Caloway's man set the scene by allowing him to go for his gun first. In a lightning twist of his body, Raider went down on his right knee and turned to face his opponent at the same time, while his Remington cleared leather on his right hip and his thumb snapped the hammer back. He plain outdrew Caloway's man, who just about had his Colt Peacemaker cocked when the Pinkerton's bullet stove in his left ribs, sending splintered shafts of bone into his heart and lungs. A great glob of blood burst from the man's mouth and rolled down his chin, dropping to his dirty gray flannel shirtfront, as he collapsed slowly onto the sawdust floor.

The backshooter's first bullet whanged off the barstool between him and the kneeling Pinkerton and buried itself in the ceiling.

He fired again, and this time the bullet cleared the barstool and tore part of Raider's shirt collar off as it passed over his shoulder and into the plank wall of the saloon, making a sound like an ax chop and splitting the plank.

Raider fired. The heavy lead .44 projectile cleared the gun barrel on a tongue of flame. The gunman had time enough to know it was on its way to him, but not the time to escape its deadly path. The force of the bullet knocked him off his feet and slapped him flat on his back, although he was a big heavy man. He lay there unmoving, eyes closed, his smoking

Schofield .45 in his right hand, a neat round red hole in the middle of his heaving belly.

It was enough to make the old man forget all about being a *mayordomo* in the *acequia* district.

The marshal had shaken Raider's hand, bought him a bottle with his own money, and had his deputies haul the two dead Caloway varmints out of the Cottonwood Inn so they wouldn't be disturbing quality folk the likes of Raider. A large-bosomed blonde in a tight-clinging silk dress attached herself to the hero of the hour. Raider looked at her big tits, which seemed ready to burst out of her low-cut dress every time she laughed, and she laughed a lot. He could see the outline of her nipples through the silky material of her tight dress. She smiled at him and suggestively rolled her tongue around her red lips.

Raider was horny as hell. He was tempted to grab her arm and take her out of the saloon to fuck her someplace right away. But here he was, with a beautiful woman in the best saloon in town, drinking liquor bought him by the marshal, listening to congratulations for having downed two gunmen at one time . . . he was a celebrity! More often than not, people glowered at him or moved away from him. Now he was everybody's friend. People admired him in Hachita! So though it was tempting to rush this beautiful blond temptress to the nearest mattress, Raider also wanted to linger a little longer in the limelight he was enjoying, to bask in his celebrity for just a short while more.

Doc Weatherbee came over to the table after he got cleaned out at the faro game. "You going to stand me a few drinks, Raider? I don't have a nickel."

"Go to the bar and order a bottle," Raider said. "I'll pay."

But Weatherbee was already pouring himself a glass from

the bottle on the table and talking with Kitty, which was the
bosomy blonde's name. Raider rooted in the pockets of his
denims, found a five-dollar gold piece, and held it out to
Doc.

"Here, take it," Raider said.

"No, you're too kind, Raider. I'll just have a few drinks
instead. I was just saying to Kitty how foolish gambling is
and how I so very rarely win at it. She tells me she's a good
cardplayer and hardly ever loses." He laughed. "I wish I'd
lost my money tonight to her instead of that shifty-eyed
riverboat character with the long thin mustachios at the faro
table."

Kitty laughed. It turned out she knew the professional
gambler at the faro table, and she described in detail some of
his tricks to Doc. She didn't even seem to notice Raider
glowering at her and Weatherbee. In another five minutes
they were so absorbed in each other that they had forgotten
him. This was it, Raider promised himself. He would let
Weatherbee have this woman. He was welcome to her. Then
he would finish working this case with him as partners, the
sooner the better. But he, Raider, was working no more cases
with this polecat, no matter what Allan Pinkerton said.
Enough was enough.

After a while Doc wondered where Raider had got to. He
hadn't noticed him leave the table, and he was nowhere to be
seen in the Cottonwood Inn. He helped Kitty with her cape
and left the saloon with her on his arm. She had a small place
on the other side of the plaza. She shivered in the chill night
air as they walked in the darkness beneath a sky full of big
bright stars.

She and Doc undressed inside her cabin by the light of the
stars coming through a high uncurtained window.

"I like the sun to stream in and wake me up with its

brightness," Kitty said. "You'll see in the morning."

"Another time, Kitty," Doc said. "I'll have to be back to the Double D before daybreak. We have trouble brewing out here."

"So I heard. Well, good luck to you if I don't find you next to me when the sun wakes me in the morning."

"You won't, but thanks all the same," Doc told her. "But I'm not rushing back to the Double D for just a little while yet." He touched the smooth skin of her side with his fingertips.

She pushed him into an upright wooden chair. Naked, she straddled his lap and played with his balls and cock, using his distended member to excite her juicy snatch. At last she guided his eager cock into her warm tight recesses. He sucked her jutting nipples and held a cheek of her ass in each hand as she bounced up and down, impaled on his mighty member. She gasped in his clutches, groaning and panting, as he wielded his shaft, which was deeply embedded in her.

She slept soundly on the bed. Doc was strongly tempted to lie beside her and sleep too. Only for a short while. But he knew he couldn't. He was a Pinkerton, and he had work to do. He put on his clothes and went out into the silent dark plaza without waking her. He saddled his horse at the livery stable, paid the stable lad, and walked his horse slowly through the starlit darkness. It was slow and difficult going until the horse reached level ground. Then it seemed to know the trail and be more sure of its footing. Doc's mount was a Double D horse that Tad had lent him, and Doc figured the animal knew its own way home. It had probably carried many a drunk ranch hand home in the dark before. He let it have its head.

Rocks, hills, and trees were black forms against the starry darkness. Out on the flatter grasslands there was little to see, though at one point he saw the crowded forms of a bunch of cattle standing quietly in the night. By the time Doc figured they should have reached the Double D ranch house, he couldn't make out any shapes that looked like the house, the barns, or the log bunkhouse. He began to lose confidence in his horse. Perhaps the animal was just wandering lost. He should definitely have come to the ranch house by now. But there was nothing Doc could do about it except ride easy in the saddle and hope for the best.

He was exhausted and half asleep in the saddle when he finally spotted the boxlike black forms of the ranch buildings some distance away. His horse plodded methodically on. Doc saw no purpose in trying to rush the animal now. It had brought him this far; it would bring him all the way. His mule Judith had him well trained as a considerate master.

Doc was still a distance from the ranch house when a voice out of the darkness startled him.

"Hold back yer hoss, fool! Stay even with the rest of us."

Another voice, more distant, spoke in a loud stage whisper. "Keep it down, boys. You can be heard for miles."

Doc reined in his animal to a very slow walking pace. He could now see the outlines of the horsemen on either side of him. He swept his derby from his head before its distinctive outlines gave him away. If they thought he was one of them he would ride with them till he got an inkling of what they were doing, though it wasn't hard for him to guess they were mounting a night attack on the ranch.

The more distant voice in the stage whisper spoke again. "Keep moving in real easy, fellas. We don't want nothing to spook them. If we come in with this half circle, blazing away when we're close, they got nothing to do but run the other way. But we gotta be right on top of them before the first shot is fired. No more talking, and I don't want to see the glow of any cigarettes. Keep all together and stay real quiet."

Doc recognized the sound of Big Pete Caloway's whisper-
g. He remembered how he and Raider had been sure the
nch was safe after sundown. Raider would have gotten
ck hours ago and be sleeping like a log right now. Doc had
give the warning before Caloway and his men got too
ose. Doc had no pistol, but there was a rifle in the saddle
abbard. He hoped it was loaded, but he couldn't be sure.
e jammed his derby back down tight on his head and drove
s heels into his horse's sides. The animal lunged forward.

"Hold back with us, fool!" the man next to him rasped.

But this time Doc kept going. He pulled the rifle from the
abbard as he urged his horse forward, worked the Win-
ester's lever action, and was relived to feel a cartridge slide
to the chamber. He fired a shot in the air, levered another
ell, fired it, and galloped as hard as he could through the
ark for the ranch house door. Shots rang out behind him,
d bullets whizzed through the air very close by. He put his
ead down on his horse's neck, crouched low in the saddle,
d pleaded with the horse to move its ass.

Panes of glass shattered in the ranch house windows and
fle barrels poked out.

"It's me! Me! Weatherbee! Don't shoot!"

Bullets from behind him were hitting the ranch house
ont wall with dry knocks. Doc jumped out of the saddle and
ttled the door. Harry Johnson opened it for him and Doc
oved fast inside, leading his horse after him.

"Hey, you can't bring a horse in here," Harry protested.

"Why not?" Doc asked indignantly. "He doesn't want to
t shot either."

With Doc's warning, they easily beat off their attackers
ith no loss on either side.

After sunup Doc said to Tad Phillips and Phil Conners,
We gotta organize ourselves and the ranch hands into a

series of watches, so that we can never be taken by surpris
day or night."

"You're gonna have trouble with the men," Phil opine
"Payday is tomorrow. I figure most of the men is going
keep riding after they hit town with their money. They s
themselves as cowpunchers, not gunfighters. The ext
money I been paying them has kept them this long, but I'
betting now they're running scared. But they'll hang in t
they get their money."

"No problem," Raider announced.

They all turned to look at him, since these were the fi
intelligible words apart from curses that the big Pinkert
had said to any of them that morning. Raider was sitting
the kitchen table, unshaven and bleary-eyed, with the emp
shells of four raw eggs before him and an empty quart be
bottle. He was working on a second quart of beer.

"Why is it no problem?" Doc Weatherbee asked a litt
testily.

"You're not going to the heart of the problem," Raid
said and belched.

"Please define the heart of the problem for us," D
requested with a sarcastic edge in his voice. "And tell
while you're at it how to approach the heart of this problem

"Surely," Raider said agreeably and took a giant slug fro
the beer bottle. "Pete Caloway is the heart of the probler
But you don't have to worry about approaching him becau
I'm going to do that for you."

Raider stood, finished off the beer, placed the bottle
the table, and belched loudly once more as he went out t
door.

Caloway was standing next to the chuckwagon drinking
tin mug of coffee when he saw the horseman on top of t
nearby hill.

"Who's that and what's he doing up there? Ain't no point being on top of that goddamn hill."

"He ain't one of ours," one of his men told Caloway. "He looks to me like that big Pinkerton son of a bitch from over on the Double D."

Caloway looked again. "I'm danged if you ain't right. But what's he doing up there? He musta gone plumb outta his mind."

While they watched, Raider calmly dismounted, tied his horse's reins to a thorn bush, and waited, standing there, looking down at the Lazy K campsite next to the burned-over patches where the ranch buildings had been.

"I think he's come to have it out with you, boss."

There was silence among the rest of Caloway's hired guns as they waited to see how their boss would react to this challenge. Caloway noted that there were no offers to take on Raider in his place. No offers to snipe at the Pinkerton with a rifle. Caloway knew that these men lived by the gun and respected an open challenge. They might shoot a man in the back when no one was looking or to help a buddy, but they also respected the courage of a lone man who could stand up and demand one-on-one single combat. Caloway was caught, and he knew it.

He went to his horse, climbed in the saddle, and moved slowly up the hill. His men stayed down below and watched him. Raider saw the tall, lean, broad-shouldered man approach and saw the familiar mean look on his pockmarked face. Raider knew what the rancher was thinking—that he had been in difficult places before and come out all right, like he was going to do this time. That's what Caloway would be saying to himself, all the while with the strong suspicion that this time things were not going to work out so well. Raider was making him climb the hill to him. Like mounting the steps of a scaffold. Raider, smiling. Calm. Sure of himself.

Big six-shooter riding on his right hip.

Pete Caloway climbed out of the saddle without a word, and his horse wandered away to join Raider's.

The two men stood face to face on the hilltop, their silhouettes outlined against the pale blue sky of the late spring morning.

"I decided you was the heart of the problem," Raider told him.

"Reckon I am," Big Pete agreed.

There was going to be no backing down on either side.

Big Pete's right hand dived for his Peacemaker. He pulled the Colt .45 out of its holster, its 4¾-inch barrel clearing the leather as its hammer was snapped back.

Raider's long-barrel .44 required a longer draw and was heavier and harder to handle than the short-barrel version of the Peacemaker. But any weapon is only what its master makes of it.

It wasn't even a close call. The Remington spat flame and barked, while the Colt never got a chance to show its stuff. Raider's bullet split Caloway's breastbone, and the hot spinning metal ripped open his heart.

When Caloway's men at the base of the hill heard the single shot and saw one figure collapse, they went resignedly about tying their bedrolls behind their saddles and moving on. This wasn't their fight.

The lone figure on the hill watched them till they were gone.

J.D. HARDIN

**"THE MOST EXCITING
WESTERN WRITER SINCE
LOUIS L'AMOUR"
—JAKE LOGAN**

___ 06572-3	**DEATH LODE #14**	$2.25
___ 06412-3	**BOUNTY HUNTER #31**	$2.50
___ 07700-4	**CARNIVAL OF DEATH #33**	$2.50
___ 08013-7	**THE WYOMING SPECIAL #35**	$2.50
___ 07017-4	**LEAD-LINED COFFINS #36**	$2.50
___ 07257-6	**SAN JUAN SHOOTOUT #37**	$2.50
___ 07259-2	**THE PECOS DOLLARS #38**	$2.50
___ 07114-6	**THE VENGEANCE VALLEY #39**	$2.75
___ 07386-6	**COLORADO SILVER QUEEN #44**	$2.50
___ 07790-X	**THE BUFFALO SOLDIER #45**	$2.50
___ 07785-3	**THE GREAT JEWEL ROBBERY #46**	$2.50
___ 07789-6	**THE COCHISE COUNTY WAR #47**	$2.50
___ 07974-0	**THE COLORADO STING #50**	$2.50
___ 08032-3	**HELL'S BELLE #51**	$2.50
___ 08088-9	**THE CATTLETOWN WAR #52**	$2.50
___ 08280-6	**MAXIMILLIAN'S GOLD #54**	$2.50
___ 08669-0	**THE TINCUP RAILROAD WAR #55**	$2.50
___ 07969-4	**CARSON CITY COLT #56**	$2.50
___ 08522-8	**GUNS AT BUZZARD'S BEND #57**	$2.50
___ 08743-3	**THE LONGEST MANHUNT #59**	$2.50
___ 08774-3	**THE NORTHLAND MARAUDERS #60**	$2.50
___ 08792-1	**BLOOD IN THE BIG HATCHETS #61**	$2.50
___ 09089-2	**THE GENTLEMAN BRAWLER #62**	$2.50

Available at your local bookstore or return this form to:

 BERKLEY
*THE BERKLEY PUBLISHING GROUP, Dept. B
390 Murray Hill Parkway, East Rutherford, NJ 07073*

Please send me the titles checked above. I enclose _____. Include $1.00 for postage and handling if one book is ordered; 25¢ per book for two or more not to exceed $1.75. California, Illinois, New Jersey and Tennessee residents please add sales tax. Prices subject to change without notice and may be higher in Canada.

NAME _____

ADDRESS _____

CITY _____ STATE/ZIP _____

(Allow six weeks for delivery.)

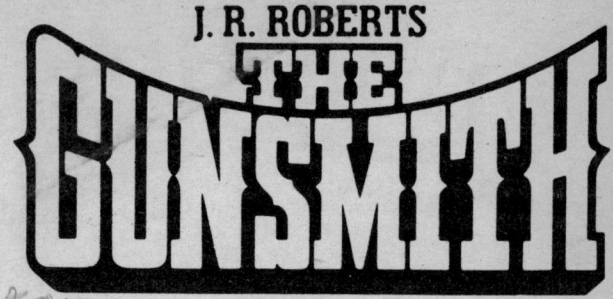

J. R. ROBERTS
THE GUNSMITH

SERIES

10 05

Prices may be slightly higher in Canada.

A1/a

a real extended holiday of this!"

They had.

That night, at midnight, it began, without a second's warning. By Friday morning it was all over. No more rockets streaking through the stratosphere, no more planes falling in flames, no more lurid lights in the sky. No nothing. Only silence, stench, and everywhere pillars of black smoke that stood mile-high into the sky, like evil genii loosed by the malice of man—upon himself.

Crouching in his rude deer blind, clutching his makeshift spear, the barefoot, hungry, heartsick little scarecrow of a man could not remember what the three-day war had been about. Certainly nothing that mattered now. No issues could possibly be that important. The war had left no victor, no vanquished, only total and tragic defeat on both sides, like two mad duelists simultaneously blowing each other's brains out in a Quixotic affair of honor that ceased, thereby, to have any discernible point or profit. It made no difference now who struck the first blow. Matters should not have been allowed to drift that far. Our rockets were launched ten seconds after the enemy's first salvo landed neatly on our hundred principal cities. Our rockets were better, the generals said.

Adam had kept the radio on in his car until he ran out of gasoline, idling the motor to keep the battery charged, so that he could listen. He heard enough to know that there had never been an armistice or any more of those murderous peace treaties. Butolinus toxin is no respecter of persons. There were no more silk-hatted diplomats left to sign anything, on either side. There was nothing resembling a government left anywhere on earth. The air, the crowded clamorous air of radio, became a silent desert several days before the car radio went dead. The last announcement on the air had croaked triumphantly that conditions on all continents and the isles of the sea were far, far worse than in the United States. After that, silence was triumphant, as power failed.

Adam raised his head and sniffed. He scented a deer, upwind on his right. His nostrils dilated. He pulled his bow-string tight and waited. It had been embarrassing, at first, to realize that the earliest and most reliable of man's five senses had been restored to him, in his hour of need. Later he had been grateful for his nose. It led to food, warned of danger.

The wind shifted and the musky scent of deer was lost. He eased his taut bowstring and sank back on his haunches. He sat like an ape and thought of God. His eyelids drooped shut. He was always tired. His nose would wake him, if anything approached. Phrases from his last sermon, the day before the End, came back. It seemed like only yester-day—and in a sense it was. He had preached that man had not ascended from the monkeys, but had descended, by ignorance and sin, from a Man who was to us as we are to the monkeys. A magnificent Proto-Man, the true image of God. And that man could evolve upward again, when he was done with warring.

Half his congregation had slept through the sermon. Now they all slept forever. And wars, apparently, were done. There being no little images of God left to wage them.

Image of God, indeed! he thought. After seeing what the image had done to God's footstool, he dreaded meeting the original. And His shining angels. Radioactive angels, no doubt. He wondered bitterly where the ancient proph-ets got their faith in superhuman beings. The songs and legends of every land seemed haunted by racial memories of a past grander than the glory of the golden age of Greece.

Had in truth a mighty race of gentle giants, wise and fair, dwelt on the sunken continent of Atlantis, fifty mil-lion years ago, leaving no trace in us but a nameless yearn-ing in the soul, an unfinished symphony torn by the winds of time? Leaving like a promise in our hearts man's para-dox of feeling pain at too much beauty? Why did men weep tears of joy, unless their blood ran bright with secret dreams of lost and greater joys? The vision of human per-fection had come from somewhere, long ago, and three thousand years of man's inhumanity had not dimmed its splendor.

Until now, of course, Adam added. Now everything was over. But it was pleasant remembering the past, in a world that had no future, and little present.

His keen ears caught a croaking sound. He sprang up ready to kill. The sound came from the brook, below. He looked down.

In the shallow headwaters of the stream, one of the queer fish lay stranded. It had grown to giant size. Nature had speeded up, as if to make up for lost time. Soon the mountain brook could not contain them. What would the resurrected proto-fish do now? Adam wondered miserably. Crawl out upon the land, develop lungs, croak lying words, organize political parties, and begin once more the obscene farce on which the curtain had fallen with a bang, these weary years ago?

Adam slid down the bank and speared the giant fish through the head. "Damn you," he said, trembling. "Don't start the whole bloody business over again!"

His wandering mind snapped into focus. A fat doe was trotting up the trail. Coming faster than usual. Something at the lower end of the valley had frightened her. Adam drew his bow, but before he could loose his arrow, the doe staggered and fell. He seized his spear and sprang over her. Then he dropped his spear and stared.

The deer was heavy with fawn, and in trouble. Adam watched as long as he could bear it. Then he put the mother out of her agony. Her dying womb released its creation. Adam covered his face with his hands. After a while he opened his fingers and peered cautiously down. Then he knelt beside it and tried desperately to make it start breathing, for it was very beautiful. It would not have been a deer at all. It was an entirely new species of hoofed mammal, fantastic, but ingeniously designed, as though by a repentant artist. It might well have survived, and flourished, and replaced the smaller race of deer, had the little doe been able to bring forth her masterpiece alive.

But it was too large.

Adam knelt and prayed, a wordless prayer, full of terrors for which there were no words. Then he buried the little mother and her strange fruit together. Badly as Mary needed meat, they could not eat of her, or it.

Scraping the loose earth noisily over the grave, Adam suddenly stopped. Another sound, far away, had reached his ear. Short and sharp. He could not guess what it had been, for he had not clearly heard it, but he sensed that it was an unnatural sound alien to the silent valley whose every breath he knew as his own. He leaped to his feet and ran down the canyon, home.

Mary was lying on her bed at the back of the dark cave. She smiled wanly as Adam burst in. "Did you call me?" he panted.

"No, but I wanted to. Adam, our boy has found some bullets. Did you hear that shot?"

Adam said, "I heard something. But it couldn't have been a shot, Mary. The firing pin on Kane's rifle was eaten away by mustard gas."

"I wish you had told me that," she said.

"I should have. But I didn't want him to start looking for a better gun. I hoped, that way, we might have a few more weeks of peace, before he—"

"No, I mean if I had known it couldn't be Kane, then I *would* have called you, Adam. Because I *did* hear a shot, far down the valley, on our side of the ridge."

"Then that means—" They faced each other in the silence of their cave. It was the moment they had dreaded, when their small secret source of food and water should be discovered by other survivors.

The heavy boots of a stranger gritted on the sunlit path outside. A ragged beast of a man was fleeing up the valley, looking back over his shoulder as if pursued. In his hand he held an army pistol. Suddenly he saw the cave, the signs of habitation around it. He rushed to the cave mouth, seized a clay crock of water, drank like a maddened animal. Then he peered into the shadowy interior his sun-blinded eyes could not yet pierce. Holding his pistol at ready, he stood in the doorway of the cave, menacing and murderous.

Adam and Mary cowered in the dark. Adam tried to raise his spear, but his arms were limp.

Kane sprang on the man from behind and drove the bayonet into his back. Falling, the man turned and fired. Kane fell across him. Then it was very still. Mary had fainted.

Adam took her pulse. It was weak, but steady.

He dragged the bodies out of the cave, where she would not see them when she awoke.

The stranger wore a tattered uniform from which the elements had long since stripped all trace of rank or nationality.

Adam looked down the canyon to see what the unknown soldier had been running from, but could sight no one. He said a prayer for Kane his son, who had been dead before he died.

From the cave, Mary called in a strained voice. "Adam, I need you!"

Adam ran back into the cave. He did what he could. Even when Mary was no longer able to tell him what to do, he seemed to know. Strength came from somewhere. But when the baby came—a beautiful, normal boy, except for his huge size, and his shimmering platinum hair—and the dark cave filled with such a gentle light as might have bathed the Manger in Bethlehem, strength left Adam Jones, and he fell to his knees weeping.

He knew then that he had lost his mind, for shining angels came and ministered unto him, and to the mother and the child.

A troop of towering, radiant young men and women, some no more than giant children, came up the path, saw the cave, and entered, lighting it as they came.

A smiling boy, whose silvery head touched the cave's high ceiling, bent down above the bed, and laughed with delight. "Look, another one of us!"

Tall girls in fair garments bathed the baby and put him

to nurse. Mary opened her eyes and watched the radiant visions she saw about her. Adam knelt by the bed, holding her hand. After a while she whispered, "Adam, am I dead?"

He whispered, "Maybe we're both dead. But listen to our baby, darling! Surely he's alive. Such a voice!"

The boy giant laughed and with one finger raised Adam to his feet. "You're not dead, friend. You're alive for the first time, today. Come down out of this animal cave and live with us. We need you dwarfs of olden time, to explain how things worked. The books are mostly gone. Not that we care. We'll write new and better books!"

The largest of the girls picked Mary up as if she were a baby, cradling her in her great graceful arms.

"You'll kill her!" cried Adam.

"Kill? We never kill," said the tall girl gently.

Mary said, "I'm quite comfortable, Adam. I want to go with them. I've hated this cave so long!"

"Then let's start," said the laughing boy. He led the way outside. Two others had buried the dead. They rolled a two-ton boulder on the double grave as easily as if it were papier-mâché. "We were after the one with the gun," they told Adam. "He needed help."

Still dazed, Adam said, "But you carry no weapons, friends. How would you have fought him?"

"Fight? We never fight," they said.

The procession moved off down the valley, through the fields of daisies shaped like orchids, through the white violets big as sunflowers, through the fields of four-leafed clover. Adam had to trot to keep up with their six-foot strides. At the ridge overlooking the rubbled graveyard that had once been Los Angeles and its suburbs, they paused to let Mary and the baby rest in the rich deep grass, a fragrant, fruited grass Adam had never seen before.

Feeling a little bolder, Adam sat down beside the oldest of them. There seemed to be no leader. They moved of a common accord, each doing what was needful, as if by instinct, or telepathy. Tremulously, Adam asked him, "Are there many like you?"

The shining countenance smiled down at him. "Not many my age," said the deep, melodious voice. "But the new crop is all ours. No more wicked little dwarfs like you, man. How could you have been so mean! I'm glad you are extinct. Look at your son—a new species, our kind. But you seem better than the few like you I've seen in cages. You're not crippled or crazy or blind. What kind of work did you do, before our time?"

"I tried to be a minister of God," said Reverend Jones humbly. "But somehow I, and my kind, failed."

"Perhaps not!" The radiant man gently laid his great hand on Adam's little one; and Adam felt a surge of joy and health and strength spread through him. The nameless yearning in his heart was stilled. The unfinished symphony of the ages rose like a mighty anthem in exquisite completion. The choking pain, the stinging tears that Adam had felt at the unbearable dreamlike beauty of these new superhuman beings dissolved in the peace that passes understanding. For the haunting glory of man's past had been found again, and the image and its Maker were one.

The glorious young man told Adam, "Come down into the valley and talk to us while we build our new city upon the ruins of the old, keeping what was good, rejecting what was bad. We want you to tell us more about this word God. We find it carved on ancient stones. There must originally have been something about you monkey-dwarfs inherently better than the poisoned mess you left behind—else you couldn't have produced mutations like us!"

With childlike pride he flexed his mighty biceps, fair and clean, threw back his great and shapely head with its mane of shimmering bright hair, and gently laughed above the new-found world, the golden laughter of an innocent young god, at life's beginning.

Some of the most exciting reading today is found in science fiction, the literature of a thousand possible tomorrows. . . .

6 Great short novels of science fiction   No. D9
Edited and with introduction by Groff Conklin

An **original** collection by six masters in the field: Stuart Cloete, Robert Heinlein, Anthony Boucher, Murray Leinster, James Blish, and Theodore Sturgeon.

"A welcome bargain whetting the appetite for a second volume."
— N. Y. Herald Tribune

384 PAGES — 35c

Outpost Mars   No. 760
by Cyril Judd

An exciting story of Earthmen on Mars. To some, it meant a second chance for man — to others, a new world to plunder.

"A human and compelling story . . ."
— San Francisco Chronicle

223 PAGES — 25c

The Best in Imaginative Storytelling

wherever pocket-size books are sold.

If these books cannot be obtained locally, send the price (plus 5c for postage and handling) for each copy to Dell Publishing Company, Inc., 10 West 33rd Street, New York 1, N. Y.